I0694099

Snowdrops and Schemes

First edition February 2026

Cover Illustrations 2026 © by Rita Evermoore

Interior Illustrations 2026 © by Rita Evermoore

All rights reserved

Library of Congress Control Number: 2025927906

ISBN 978-1-966851-04-2 (tr. pbk.)

ISBN 978-1-966851-05-9 (hardcover)

ISBN 978-1-966851-06-6 (ebook)

Published by Whispering Cloak Press

SNOW DROPS AND SCHEMES

By
Rita Evermoore

To the magic in all of us

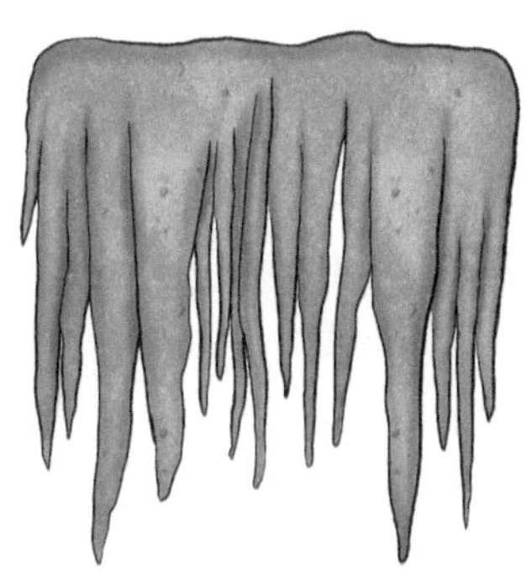

Chapter One

I saw sprites in the icicles as the train rumbled through the Alps. Ronnie lay curled up in the chair beside me, her head on my shoulder. She'd insisted on coming with me instead of staying behind in Coldwater. She'd said the foundation could take care of itself while we were gone.

I think she was worried I would get into some kind of trouble, or maybe she just didn't see it as fair that I would get to meet B and she wouldn't. After all, I had high hopes he would teach me magic. I couldn't blame her for wanting the same after losing her mentor. It would be nice to have a piece of home with me in the cold mountain peaks and plunging valleys.

For some reason, I'd found it nearly impossible to sleep on the plane, and it appeared the train would be no better. At least there was far more to see rushing through the Alpine scenery. Besides, I'd been neglecting my blog in preparation for the trip. It was high time I got back into it.

I had to take advantage of the Wi-Fi while I had it. Our next train would be much smaller, and it was unlikely to have internet connection at all. I tried not to bother Ronnie as I began to type.

My blog hadn't amounted to much yet, but it was a start. At the very least it was a place to set out my thoughts and work through what had happened and what I had done. Perhaps it was foolish to share my notes with the world. Perhaps I should have kept them to myself, but maybe I *was* a fool.

Field notes (travel):

Welcome to my little travel log. I hope you follow me on my trip and that maybe we can learn something together. I am currently writing from a train in the Swiss Alps, as I am on my way to a small mountain town, the name of which I will keep to myself for the safety of those I meet there. We (my friend Ronnie is here too, snoring away on my shoulder) have a new friend we will meet when we get there.

I have begun my paper notes and am moving some of my thoughts onto this blog for you all to enjoy. Starting off, I want to talk about Alpine mythology and the creatures therein. I have done a decent amount of research on these creatures that compose Alpine legend, and three fabled beings stand out to me to start: the primordial mountain giants, the deceptive mist maidens, and the helpful house-hold spirits.

Mountain Giants: These are primordial giants that are big, strong, and simple-minded: Gargantua (Old Gargy) is their king, Hotap is the one who eats humans, Bertha his daughter, and Schopp is the personification (or I guess giantification?) of imbibing too much.

Gargantua is kind and slow, yet allegedly responsible for raising the famous Matterhorn to its current height. What happened to such an enormous creature? Furthermore, if he did die of old age as legends say, what happened to his colossal skull? Surely there would be some sort of evidence, would there not?

Undines: These water nymphs, or mist maidens, are of particular interest to me as we are going to one of many towns that sit in a valley surrounded by waterfalls. I imagine there are plenty of stories about the beautiful women who inhabit such waters.

The Undine are a fascinating subsect of nymphs found in springs and freshwater streams that have the ability to become human when they marry a human man. However, they are tethered to him and, if he is ever unfaithful, she will die, or so the story goes.

Kobolds: This group of creatures is a favorite of mine. I say "group" because this is a larger umbrella classification that encompasses more than one particular creature. These ghibli-esqe spirits are household servants. They are found in many different cultures by many different names: boggart, brownie, gobeline, nisse, tomte, duende, trasgu, and domovoi, just to name a few, for the list goes on and on.

Kobolds and the other cultural variants have a tendency for a little fun and trickery, but if they like you, they might just deign to make your house as cozy as could be. Perhaps I will meet some of them tucked away in this idyllic village.

We are nearly at the next train station and I doubt I will have Wi-Fi for a while (as our host is a little old-fashioned) but I promise to update you as soon as I can.

Believe with all your heart,

Amber

The train slowed as a voice came from the speakers, first in German, then Italian, French, and English. I was barely paying attention when I started to understand the words.

Ronnie lifted her head from my shoulder and looked around. "Are we there?"

"Almost." I closed my laptop. "Ours is the next stop. Then we get on a smaller train and we'll be in Neblig before you know it."

"Oh wow!" Ronnie looked past me out the window. "It's beautiful out there. You should have woken me."

"Last time I did that, you took a swipe at me." I chuckled.

"Last time you did that, it was dark outside and we weren't passing so many gorgeous snow-topped mountains." She pulled out her camera and leaned over me to snap a couple pictures.

"I can never win, can I?"

"Nope." Ronnie smirked at me. "Though it might be helpful to know I'm way more interested in beautiful sights than I am in airplane food."

"Duly noted." No matter what happened, I was happy Ronnie was there. Traveling outside the country alone would have been pretty daunting.

"How you feeling about meeting B?" Ronnie asked, as if she could read my mind. Or maybe she just read my face.

"Excited mainly. Though I'd be lying if I said I wasn't nervous. After all, we barely know anything about him. Letters are such an inefficient means to get to know someone, and it's only been . . . what, four months?"

"That's why we're going to see him though." Ronnie ran her fingers through her silky hair. "We'll have plenty of time to get to know him and honestly, what's the worst that can happen?"

"He could be like Ms. Avery, or worse," Sadness said.

"What if he's only bringing us here to eat us? Or to use us for his magic?" Creativity squealed, more excited than scared.

"That's ridiculous," Literal countered. *"What good would we be to him? It's far more likely that he actually hates Ms. Avery and is looking to enact his revenge on us since she is gone."*

"Now who's being ridiculous?" Creativity spat. *"He was one of the few who even responded to our letters about Ms. Avery passing, and he's been kind this whole way."*

"Amber?" Ronnie tapped me on the shoulder. "Are you alright? I was just joking about the worst thing happening, but it'll all be fine. I'm sure of it. B has been nothing but kind, and he's going to teach us . . ." he glanced around the train car, then whispered, ". . . about magic."

"Yes, very comforting because our track record on mentors is sooo stellar." I pushed my thoughts down and tried to stay present with her. "But no, you're right. I'm just in my head about this. You know me, always thinking."

Ronnie grinned. "One of us has to do the thinking, and I'm glad it isn't me."

Announcements started blaring, and they'd only gotten to French by the time people started to stand up and collect their luggage from the racks. Ronnie jumped out of her seat and grabbed our bags. She lifted them both and wouldn't allow me to take mine when I reached for it.

"I've got the bags. You've got enough to carry with all those heavy thoughts." She laughed and shuffled off the train. "My thoughts are so light I'll lift off the ground without the weight. So you're really doing us both a favor."

The train station was stupidly easy to navigate as there were only two terminals, the main line we were getting off and the much smaller one that ran out into the middle of nowhere. I had to admit I was happy for the change of scenery. There was no denying Coldwater was wonderful in its own way, but I'd been cooped up in Ms. Avery's study for so long that I felt as if I were going mad. She had so much stuff to sort through.

We passed the second train ride uneventfully, and both of us were happy to sit and watch the wonderful views outside our window.

"He'll be waiting for us on the platform, I think?" I said, finally breaking the silence.

"Was that a question or a statement?"

"A bit of both, I suppose." I kept running through the events that were to unfold. Neblig was no doubt different in my mind than reality, as was B. Even still, it didn't keep me from thinking it all through.

"How many times do I need to reassure you that everything's going to be alright?"

"Yeah, I know it will." I nodded, but it didn't help my restless mind much.

The train chugged into the station, and everyone scurried to get their bags. I didn't even try snagging mine. It was a futile effort with Ronnie there.

Only one person stood on the platform looking up at the train as the doors opened. A few other passengers got off with us, but no one waited for them. They quickly disappeared into the town, leaving us with the tall, lithe, platinum-blond tree of a man who looked far too young and far too handsome to be B.

"Ms. Dawson and Ms. Veyl, I presume?" the young man said. I couldn't place his accent. It didn't sound Swiss-German, French, or Italian. It didn't sound like a mix of any of them either.

"He's so regal . . . and those cheekbones." Lure swooned.

"That's us." Ronnie stepped forward when I didn't answer right away. "You must be B. I'm Ronnie. Nice to meet you." She dropped her bag and reached out to shake his hand.

B shook her hand but looked over her shoulder at me. "So you are the one I've been corresponding with—the writer."

I darted forward and took his hand as he was pulling it away from Ronnie. I kicked myself internally for the awkwardness but couldn't go back. "Yes, that's me. Nice to meet you." My head reeled as my image of who B was collided with the real-life version of him, and they didn't align at all. "You're tall. And young."

B let out a crystalline laugh. "I see that you are much more a writer than a talker. And yes, I am tall, but as for the second, well, looks can be deceiving." His bluntness felt like a refreshing punch in the face. "Come now, we have a bit of a walk to my house. Let me take those." He grabbed our bags from Ronnie and began walking out of the station.

I glanced over at Ronnie, fully expecting her to protest, but she looked as mesmerized with how different B was as I felt. I nudged her, and we shared a knowing look before following our new acquaintance.

He'd undersold how long a walk it was—and how steep. By the time we reached his house, I felt as though it would have been better to just sleep in the train station. I was going to get in better shape simply walking to town and back. It didn't even seem to faze B. He must have been used to the strenuous exercise.

"Welcome to my home," B said from up ahead. "I'll get you ladies comfortable in your rooms before taking you on a walking tour of town—if you are up for it. Oh, and maybe some food too. That would be good."

Snow crunched under my feet, and my breath hung in the air, heavy from the climb as B's home came into view. The cottage seemed to grow out of the side of the mountain, its rustic beams and cream-colored exterior a quintessential Alpine style. Flickering firelight shone through bubbled glass windows, like a cottage in a Christmas village set. It made me want to curl up by the fire and read a book.

"How long have you lived here, B?" I asked. In our letters, he'd never been all that forthcoming. I had hoped he would be different in person.

"A good long while. However, I have a couple of homes in different countries. But this is one of my favorites." His voice grew wistful. "Though my winter home in Norway is the oldest." His words were exacting, as if speaking English for our benefit wasn't easy. I may not need to look much further for a good mystery than our host.

He led us up to the cottage, which loomed larger and larger as we grew near. It was less a cottage and more a mansion, with different architecture denoting additions to it through the years.

The front was a modern chalet style, but behind it was older stone architecture.

"*Does anyone know what years these might have been built in?*" The Originator asked.

"*The front with all of the large glass windows looks modern,*" Literal said.

"*You're a genius,*" Creativity scoffed.

"*Okay then, what do you think?*" Literal scowled.

"*I think there is a cave in those rocks behind the house, and that is where the house actually started.*"

Literal blew Creativity a raspberry.

I made a note to do some more research on architectural periods in the Alps. And though the styles were different, whoever had made the additions did a great job of melding them together. Perhaps B had done it himself.

He led us through a carved wooden door into a softly lit hallway. The ceiling was a bit higher than I was used to, no doubt to accommodate B's height. I couldn't call him willowy as he was too muscular for that, but he did look strangely delicate in proportions due to his height.

The tops of the walls were trimmed in blue and silver, which cascaded down to earthy greens and browns near the floor. It mimicked the Alps with their snow-covered peaks and verdant new spring greenery.

I smelled something hearty cooking in the kitchen and wondered, for the first time, if B lived with someone else. He'd never mentioned anyone, and I'd assumed he'd lived a solitary life like Ms. Avery, but perhaps I was wrong. Or perhaps he had another visitor.

"Who's cooking?" I couldn't help myself.

B turned back toward us and said. "Amethyst. You'll meet her in a little bit, but I want to get you settled first."

"Is she your wife?" I pressed.

B laughed. "No, I have no wife." He turned into a side hallway going back toward what I presumed was the older portion of the house. "And I have no other attachments either, if that is your next question," he said over his shoulder.

I hadn't planned on asking him about that but was glad of the answer nonetheless. He dropped Ronnie off in her room first and I was a little jealous when she didn't have to walk as far, but that was soon curbed.

"I figured you would like to be closer to the library," B said, gesturing inside what would be my room for the next few weeks. "If you drop off your things, I can show it to you before we go on our walk."

"That's so . . . thoughtful of you." I felt bad about being ungrateful. After all, he didn't have to agree to host us, and he was so genuinely interested in what we cared about. I dropped my stuff and barely looked inside before following him.

The library's door was even more ornate and detailed than the front one. It showed where B's priorities lay, and I couldn't help but respect him for it.

He pulled the heavy doors open as if they were nothing and led me into a dimly lit room. Fear sprang to life in my chest for the briefest of moments. *Did I miscalculate? I never should have let him separate us.*

"Ms. Dawson, are you alright?" B's cool hands gripped my shoulders, steadying me.

"I ah . . ." Embarrassment flushed my cheeks and I was glad he couldn't see. "Yes, I'm fine, but can we have some more light?"

"Oh, of course." I heard nerves in his tone as the room lit up with fiery blue light.

Little orbs danced among the shelves, and I thought I saw humanoid shapes within them. They shone, illuminating towering stacks of books as far as I could see in a massive cave. Musty books perfumed the air.

"*Told you.*" Creativity laughed.

"You keep books in a cave?" I said in horror. "How do they not get damaged?"

B laughed. "Don't worry, my magic is strong enough to protect them. Only this cave was big enough to house them all. Although, the truly old volumes reside in my other homes—in bigger libraries."

I glanced at all the shelves and took in a sharp breath. A library larger than these thirty-foot stacks would be truly massive. I *had* to see them. There were cushioned chairs among the stacks and, though the room was cold, I could imagine what it would be like once a fire was set in the hearth.

"What are they?" I nodded to the lights. "I've never seen anything like them."

"Spirits who like my library enough to illuminate it for me and help maintain it when I am gone."

Finding magical creatures around B was going to be easier than I thought. I looked up at him, his face tinged blue by the spirits' glow. I was still getting used to the reality of fantasy. It was all around me, hidden in plain sight.

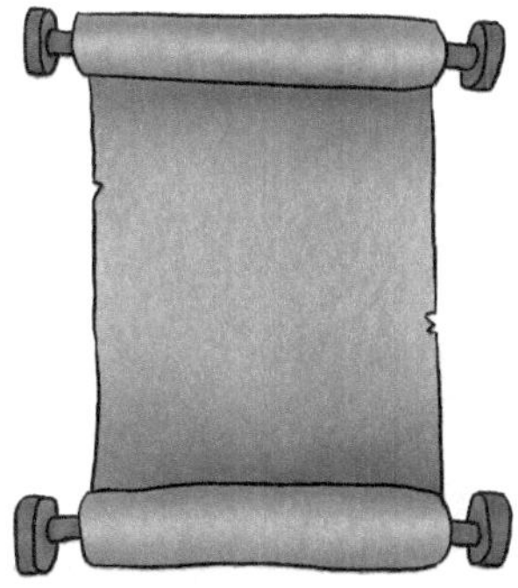

Chapter Two

I COULD UNDERSTAND THE blue floating spirits and their desire to reside in B's extensive library. He had so many volumes, and they perfumed the air with their scent. It mingled with an earthy odor coming from farther in.

I walked deeper into the shelves, and the tile floor slowly transitioned to smooth stone. B's house held mysteries beyond him.

"Man, you'd give Ms. Avery a run for her money with these books." I looked at all the leather-bound tomes and could feel how old they were. I wanted so very much to touch them, but I wouldn't without his permission.

"I've had a lot longer to grow my collection than Ms. Avery had." He brushed his fingers along the books' spines as I'd wanted to. "You are more than welcome to read any book in my collection. I know all too well how terrible it is to leave one's books behind. The truly ancient specimens I own are in my home in Norway. In fact, many of them aren't even books as you know them."

"What do you mean?" I still worried about touching the books. I should wash my hands first.

"I have quite a few scrolls and tablets. Some wooden and some stone. You'll have to come visit me when I'm there, though I must admit that I am much busier in wintertime. You'll see less of me, but my home is open." He smiled and handed me a book, no doubt noting my apprehension.

"Why open up your house at all?" The way it came out sounded ungrateful in my ears. I tried again. "What I mean is—do you open your homes to guests often?"

B shook his head and leaned against the stone wall amid the stacks. "Not as often as I used to. I have to be careful who I show all of this to. Some people would try to steal what I have, and others just wouldn't understand it. So many things have changed through the centuries. That's why I see so much hope in you, Ms. Dawson."

"Amber. Please call me Amber. It makes me feel like a little girl, calling me Ms. Dawson."

He nodded. "My apologies, Amber." He said my name as though he were tasting it. "As I was saying, you give me hope in that you seem set on bringing about a renaissance of fantastical acceptance with your writings. Though I must say I am not nearly as optimistic as you are on the subject. I've found that most people in this world are not open to things they don't understand and can't control. Still, if you are able to even bring a fair few of us out of hiding, it will be more than we have accomplished in some good long time. You are prudent in maintaining our anonymity, and I imagine you will keep our secrets as you discover more in my parts of the world."

I nodded, grateful that he'd taken the time to read some of my blog and approved of it. I had so many questions. "Do the people of Neblig know about our reality?"

"Some, though on the whole, I would say not." B moved toward the door and I put the book back, following after. "Most of us supernaturals live outside of town. Though, of all the places to settle, Neblig has more lore and more superstition than most places. If any town was going to truly see and believe what is out there, it would be a place like Neblig. I've often thought of Ms. Avery in Coldwater and what she was trying to do ther . . . or, from what your letters suggest, what she gave up doing."

Ronnie popped out of her doorway just as we arrived at her room. "We're doing our best to continue that work," Ronnie said, as if she'd been part of the conversation all along. "Ms. Avery did a lot of work before she . . . uh . . . lost her way, and Amber's doing a great job going through and trying to make sense of her writing and plans, but it's taking time."

"I'm sure she's doing a wonderful job." B smiled at me. "Now, we should get on with our walk before it gets dark. Amethyst will never let me hear the end of it if we aren't back in time for dinner." He muttered under his breath a little dialogue where Amethyst seemed to be berating him for not showing up in time for a dinner for which he'd picked the time. He sounded like a child.

Once outside, I asked, "B, how old are you?" I was tired of beating about the bush and being scared of asking my questions. If he found them offensive, he'd just have to tell me so.

"After so many centuries, one stops counting. Let's just say that I am quite old. Far older than Ms. Avery or most of my acquaintances, no matter how long-lived." He seemed sad, which was understandable. If he was older than most he knew, then he'd lost many people along the way.

To me, B appeared as a man in his late twenties. I wondered if he could change his appearance, living through a full life cycle before starting young again. It was the only way I could think that he would be able to continue living in the same place year after year.

He was rather handsome, with long white-blond hair and delicate pale features. I could believe that he hailed from Norway, from the Vikings. He almost looked like an elf from *Lord of the Rings*—handsome, but also beautiful.

The trip down from B's house was far easier than the trip up, but it was still a long way. By the time we reached the bottom, most of the valley was covered in long mountain shadows.

"What is there to do in Neblig?" Ronnie asked. "I did actually try to look up things to do here, but I didn't find much. Other than the fact that Neblig is a cozy retreat and that you'd probably have to leave for any excitement. Is that true?"

"It depends." B led us into town. We passed a small school where children played on a public playground with their parents, yelling and laughing while they crunched through the melting snow. "Most people go to the more popular parts of the Alps, but we get a few people here for a more relaxing sort of vacation. After all, we don't have cars here, and it's a little bit like stepping back in time. That's part of why I love it so much. The world moves much too fast for my taste nowadays. But you have come to Neblig at a good time. We have a festival soon."

"Oh yes!" I exclaimed. "I read about that. Chalandamarz, a spring festival about waking good spirits and warding off the bad."

B grinned. "That is right. I should have expected nothing less from a writer than to do her research. Chalandamarz is one of Neblig's big festivals. It marks the official end of winter and is the first day of March. That is the literal translation from the Romansch language. It is a fun tradition, and even some of the most natural creatures attend from the sidelines, so in a way the festival works."

"Most natural?" Ronnie voiced my question.

"It's my way of saying supernatural. For you, it may seem super-natural, but I know it is the essence of nature. It is more natural than most, for it is more ancient and tied to deep natural func-tionality."

I tried to think of it from his point of view. Surely, anything that existed was technically nature. *Perhaps my thinking is a little more human-centered than it ought to be.*

My thoughts were interrupted by the beauty of the town. It was one thing to look out over the village dusted white with fading snow, and it was another to smell the pine sap and baking fill the air.

"It smells like pretzels." I followed the scent to a nearby bakery and pressed my face to the glass, only to see darkness within. "Aw man, it's closed."

I contented myself with peering in the window filled with decorated cakes, lavish tarts with rich custardy filling, and flaky pastries galore. It made me think of Harper and the bakery. Ronnie had done so much work in getting it operational in the past few months. "Yes, they bake overnight," B said. "So they are probably just getting started. It is a great place to have breakfast. You will find that we have no shortage of places to eat. It is one of Neblig's favorite pastimes."

I spun around in the street and took in the rows of shops and people scurrying between them. They wore warm wool sweaters, but a fair few weren't wearing coats. I couldn't imagine not being cold in that moment as the wind whipped down the main street.

B led us farther down the street toward a square with a fountain. The buildings were larger now, with four main ones on the corners showcasing ornate carved woodwork and a rustic charm. The cold only made the thought of going inside the shops more enticing.

"Oh, hot chocolate." I stepped toward the little cart and called back, "Ronnie, do you want some?"

"Do you even have to ask?"

I glanced at B, who nodded, before dashing over to the older man. He poured the thick liquid from a carafe into a paper cup that puffed steam and already had three drinks ready for me by the time I produced the francs to purchase them.

"This truly is a beautiful place." I stood in the center of town and where the two main roads crossed and saw four waterfalls roaring in all directions. They weren't very loud from so far away, but I could see what looked like icicles at the top and on the rocks to the sides. "I can understand why you've stayed here for so long."

"How long have you been here?" Ronnie asked. "I'm not sure how all of that works."

I worried that B would get mad that we were talking about something so delicate in town, but he didn't seem bothered at all. He led us over to a large store where two men chatted, away from other people. I wondered how they were just sitting there rocking in the chilly air but had to remind myself that it was spring for them. Even if I was cold, the locals probably weren't.

"Longer than this town," B said before turning to the men. "Bastien and Jetmir, I want you to meet Ms. Amber Dawson and Ms. Ronnie Veyl. They are going to be staying with me for the next few weeks, and I want you to look out for them while they're here."

"B, old friend, you're making it out as though we usually tar and feather our visitors," Bastien said with a laugh. "Don't worry, girls. This town is safe as can be." He was a little older with a long silver shaggy beard and scarred hands.

"Yeah, the only dangerous thing around here is Bastien's music." Jetmir chuckled. "Pray you never have the displeasure of hearing it." Jetmir looked middle-aged and ruggedly handsome with a scruffy beard and piercing blue eyes that had crows feet dug deep into them. It was clear he was fond of laughing, and that Bastien gave him plenty of opportunity to do it.

"Is anyone else about?" B asked, clearly amused by their antics. "Or are we stuck with just you fools for Amber's and Ronnie's introductions to Neblig?"

"Aelyn and Nisse are home," Jetmir said. "Probably making dinner, I'd think."

"What about Branson, is he eating with them tonight?" B asked.

"Could be," Jetmir answered. "Not sure though. He said he had a couple of things to do tonight. Who knows what is going on with that one." His nose scrunched almost imperceptibly.

"Alright. Well, good seeing you, boys. We have to get a move on. It's already getting pretty dark."

Bastien tipped his head to us, and Jetmir waved goodbye. Ronnie and I followed B, and I wondered if those two knew more about B than most. After all, he did interact with them as if he were older than them.

"I'm afraid you've already seen most of Neblig," B said, as we walked away from the center of town. We passed some more restaurants, and my stomach growled at the scent of grilled meat and buttery things. "Maybe you can explore town more tomorrow morning."

I sipped my hot chocolate, and it warmed me from within. Couples passed in fine dresses and coats as they ducked into warmly lit restaurants. The bustle was slow; everyone moved with an ease that was calming even in its motion.

"If you need anything, Jetmir and Bastien are the two to go to. If they don't have something at their store, they'll know where to get it." He paused and then said, "We have one more stop before we have to head home. I don't want to make Amethyst upset. That never turns out well for me."

"Is the house both of yours?" I asked.

"Sort of," B shrugged. "She lives there year-round. It's her home more than it is mine, and she's kind enough to take care of me when I'm in town, but let's not talk about her here."Before I had time to say anything else or even think much, we stood in front of a three-story building made from the same logging wood as the rest of town, but it had ornate wooden overhangs like a ski chalet and was painted a pale blue that made it stand out among the cream and brown buildings. B knocked on the door.

I heard footsteps from within and the clinking of utensils. The door pulled open, and a young woman, close in age to Ronnie and me, looked out. She was blonde, with curves accentuated by the green apron tied at the waist.

"Aelyn," B said.

"B, to what do I owe this surprise?" Aelyn asked. "Truth be told, I didn't know you were back. It's a little early, no?" Her accent almost sounded French, but not quite. It was closer to B's accent than anything. In fact, as I looked back and forth between them, I could see some small resemblance in their features.

"*Brother and sister?*" Creativity asked.

"*No, she lives in town.*" Literal scoffed. "*Surely, if she was B's sister, she would live away from town for safety. She might be his kid, though. Half human so she doesn't fit in within town or outside of it.*"

"*Kid?*" Lure crawled out from wherever she'd been daydreaming. "*Who said anything about him having kids?*"

"*Oh come off it, Lure.*" Creativity laughed. "*Don't be so naive. Of course B has had kids. He's ancient. Ancient things like having kids. Besides, why do you even care?*" Creativity taunted.

"*I don't.*" Lure crossed her arms and sank back into softness, trying not to be noticed.

Sadness took notes. "*So she could be his kid, or sister—*"

"*Or a squirrel,*" Inner Child cut in.

"*A squirrel?*" The rest of them turned to her.

"*Yes.*" Inner Child's voice was small. "*She could have been a squirrel. Maybe B enchanted her to be a woman. That's probably why she's so pretty. You could be as beautiful as you want as a human if you used to be a squirrel.*"

"Amber." I felt Ronnie's hand on my arm. "Amber, he asked you a question."

I looked around and noticed that we were no longer outside and I hadn't taken my coat off, so I was rather warm. I looked over at

B, assuming he was the "he" Ronnie had meant, but he nodded toward another man with a square jaw, hefty build and shock of shaggy black hair.

"What was the question? Sorry, my thoughts carried me away for a moment." I flushed a little. Ronnie said I'd been disappearing into my mind a lot lately, but it was different when it was just the two of us.

"No worries." The man, who I presumed was Nisse, smiled, making his already kind eyes look even kinder. "I was just asking about your writing. What sorts of things do you write? You seem to have impressed B, which in terms of stories is quite the feat."

I flushed further. I was sure my face was bright red. "Well, I don't know what B's been saying, but he was unfortunate enough to see the first draft of my latest manuscript. So surely he's lying."

"Oh, B doesn't do that." Aelyn laughed. "He's as truthful as they come."

It was B's turn to blush. "I think it's time for us to return home. Amethyst is waiting for us."

"So soon?" Aelyn pouted. "Branson will be by any minute. He'll want to meet your new friends. Here, let me take those—I'll get you fresh ones while we wait." She took our disposable cups of cocoa and disappeared into the house.

I looked at B, who was a little uncomfortable but hid it well. Fortunately we didn't have to wait long. After a few minutes, there was a knock at the door and Nisse went and answered it.

"Branson, come on in. You're not our only guest tonight." Nisse led a lanky man wearing a crisp brown suit into the room. His hair was cut short and gelled perfectly in place.

"Hello," the newcomer said. "And who are your friends . . . B?"

"Amber and Ronnie. They are friends from America." He stood and shook Branson's hand. "How have you been this autumn and winter? Not causing too much trouble, are you?"

Branson laughed and pulled B into a hug. When they released each other, he made a point to brush out all the wrinkles in his suit until it was crisp again.

Aelyn reappeared with hot chocolate. She handed me a mug, and I took a sip. It was rich, dark, and put the other one to shame. I wanted to enjoy it, but B was getting antsy, so I drank it down quickly.

"Now we really do have to go," B said, and set his mug on the side table.

"Are you sure? We have plenty to eat here." Aelyn was eager to keep us there. "And Branson's only just arrived."

"I'm afraid so. Amethyst probably already has food waiting for us at home." B stood and swung his coat on. "We've already pushed our luck. The only thing that might keep me from a proper scolding is the presence of my guests."

"Well, it was very nice meeting both of you." Aelyn reached out to hug Ronnie and me. I let her embrace me, but I regretted it. She must have spilled something on her apron, because it was all wet and the texture felt awful.

"It was nice to meet you, too." I tried to keep my cringing from coloring my voice and turned away to follow B so she couldn't see my face.

It had grown colder outside, but I was sweating by the time we got back to B's house. He led us in, and we put our coats on the hooks by the door before entering a warmly lit dining room. The space was much larger than I'd expected. Perhaps he hosted more than I thought.

A hearty meat pie waited, steaming on the table. I looked around for Amethyst, but didn't see her. *She must still be in the kitchen.*

"Amethyst, I'm sorry, dear." B looked over to the head of the table and for a moment I thought Amethyst might have been invisible, until she hopped up on a chair.

She was small, no taller than two feet, and looked both old and young at the same time. Her eyes were large and round, and her nose was short and squashed. Her hair was hidden in a cap, if she had any hair at all, and she wore a simple frock and apron.

"You'll be the death of me," she griped. Her voice was more childlike than gritty and more than a little bit stern. "I know you control a great deal, but you can't ever be on time. What would your mother think?" She shook her head and started serving the food, even though none of us were seated.

"I don't have a mother." B grinned at her.

Amethyst was a kobold. That much was clear. It wasn't just will-o'-the-wisps in the library; B's house was flush with the fantastical.

A kobold, will-o'-the-wisps—but what was B?

Chapter Three

I WOKE TO THE smell of lavender. Beside me on the table was a steaming cup of tea. I glanced around searching for Amethyst or B but found neither. I listened for footsteps, but there were none.

"Ooh, the house made us tea!" Inner Child squealed, waking me fully.

"Amethyst probably made it," Literal responded.

"And just how did she know that we would be getting up or that we wanted lavender tea?" Creativity asked.

"'Cause she's magic." Inner Child giggled. *"Who cares, I want tea and to explore the house. Ooh, maybe the kitchen is set up just for Amethyst to be able to reach everything. I'd really like something my size like that."*

The others all shared knowing inklings, but none of them felt the need to tell her.

I sat up in bed and shoved some pillows behind me so I could sip my tea comfortably. The room was decorated in furs and dried flowers. Perhaps they had been fresh last spring.

After last night's walk and supper with B and Amethyst, my mind was reeling. There were a great many questions. I hadn't expected to encounter so much magic in so little time. I didn't know why, but I had figured B would ease us into it. Although now that I had gotten to interact with him, it didn't really seem like B's style.

I knew I should work on my blog while I could. I was here to learn about magic, yes, but also to record my findings, so I had to sneak in some writing sessions periodically. As I sat there, however, I realized I didn't have Wi-Fi. So I settled on starting a new novel in my notebook. After all, this wasn't just about research; it was also a retreat from all the craziness of home.

It took everything in me to get out of bed, put on a thick, fluffy robe that was already in the guest room, and head outside rather than to the library. I'm sure B wouldn't have minded me visiting the library, as he had been the one to show it to me, but I needed to take in the Alpine sights.

It was much warmer in the morning sun than it had been on our trek up the mountain the previous night, a fact for which I was grateful. I could still feel the end of winter shaking out its fur and growling at the springtime sun.

I found a rock to sit on, looking down over the valley, and set a fur on it before sitting. There were the beginnings of flowers poking out from the ground all around the rock. Their bulbs told them it was time to see the sun, even with the bit of snow still on the ground.

I worried that my pen had grown rusty as I'd sorted out Ms. Avery's affairs. Fortunately, as I looked within, I found the ideas waiting. They greeted me as old friends might.

What does it mean to be human, to be a god? *Nessi thought as she washed her clothes in the river. She was beginning to give up hope of ever finding humans and understanding what it might mean to be one.*

"What's on your mind, little one?" Beast asked as he dragged a stag into their small camp.

"How can you be something properly without knowing anyone else who is like you?" She laid her dress on a rock to dry and went back to tending the fire.

"Instinct." Beast growled as he began ripping into his meal, making sure to leave a large chunk for her to roast over the fire. "I don't know anyone else like me, but I know I need food and how to catch it, and I believe that means it's an instinct. No one taught me to do it. I'm just me and you are just you, little bird."

"I wish you wouldn't call me little all the time," Nessi fretted. "I want to be big and strong. Maybe I don't want to be little Nessi anymore."

Beast got up from his meal and came to sit next to her by the fire so she could braid her fingers in his fur. "Don't wish away a person I love."

I pulled myself away from the story. It was a good place to stop, and the others would probably wake soon. But as I set aside my notebook and pen, my eyes were drawn to the town below. It was filled with activity surrounding a central square. Most of the snow had melted overnight as it grew unnaturally warmer.

"You're up early." B's voice came from behind me. I jumped.

"Don't do that. You could have sent me down the mountain permanently."

"Not to worry, I would have caught you." He seemed perfectly serious.

I tilted my head but didn't engage. "Is there something going on today in town? For the festival perhaps?"

"Not that I'm aware of. May I?" He gestured to the open piece of pelt beside me.

I nodded.

"They don't always tell me what is going on in town. And as you no doubt heard Aelyn say, I have only just gotten back here, and earlier than usual."

"Did you come back earlier just for us?" I felt warmth spread across my chest. It felt nice to be important.

"I'll admit that you were a part of it, but not the whole. I have some other business to attend to that brought me south."

"And are you going to tell me about this business, or am I free to let my imagination run wild?"

"I think we'll have to let your imagination handle this one. I'm sure it's up to the test." He paused for a moment, looking out over the mountains before asking, "Why did you say you aren't a good writer?"

"Because I'm not." I picked up my journal and held it to my chest. I don't know why I did it.

"But I read the story you sent me about the girl and the wolf. It was beautiful. You are much better than you think. Perhaps you need someone outside of yourself to show you that."

"I appreciate it, though I still don't agree." If I were honest with myself, I was in a bit of a writerly slump. The manuscript hadn't really gone anywhere. I thought I'd made some real strides in improving my writing, but others didn't seem to think I had what it took. I was a fraud if I called myself an author. It might be silly to continue her story, but it's what I wanted to write.

"You'll see it eventually." His voice came out like wind whispering against my ear. I almost didn't think he'd actually said anything.

We sat in silence for a while. I watched the bustle of town and people congregating in the square until finally, I noticed that there were too many people.

"What *are* they doing?" I couldn't help myself. I was curious.

"Well, there's only one way to find out. We should go down and see." He popped up and looked back at me.

I stood, saying, "I should go wake Ronnie. She'll kill me if I let her miss all the fun, even if I have to wake her up. For that, she might just scold me."

As soon as I stood up, B snatched the fur from the rock. At first, I thought he was mad I had put it there, but then I saw him smirk. *Perhaps some sort of chivalry?*

I didn't fight him on it, but I didn't give in to whatever he was doing either, no matter how much Lure might want to. That wasn't what I was in Switzerland for. Plus, that hadn't worked out well the last time, and it could only be a hundred times worse with a man who was god knows how old. I didn't even know what he was, but B definitely wasn't human.

"You think a lot," B said as we reached the front door.

"What?"

"You disappear for long stretches of time. Are all writers like this?" B had a childlike wonder about him. It was an odd thing for one so old, but when I really thought about it, it made a lot of sense. Humans are most like children in old age, when they've lost the strictures of societal expectations. Surely, an ancient being would experience something similar.

"I can't speak for all writers, but I guess I would say that adjusting to being around people more is causing some difficulty; before I went to Coldwater and met Ronnie and Ms. Avery, I had to steal my solitude. I lived with my parents and often disappeared into my thoughts. My mom used to yell at me for not being present with her." I moved on from *that* topic quickly. "Over the last few months, I've spent a lot of time alone with my thoughts, and they do keep me in good company."

B nodded and his face was serious, as if he resonated with at least part of what I'd said. "I used to write too. But that was a long time ago. Some of my poems have survived out in the human world, but most of them only live on in libraries like mine. Eclectic mixes of the art of people I once knew and the person I once was."

"Do you know everyone whose books are in your library?" It was such an intriguing notion.

"No, not all of them. But I do have some rare gems that I'm glad I hung onto because they probably wouldn't have survived otherwise."

I couldn't help wondering what items other ancient beings had held onto. Relics, books, artifacts. We'd barely even talked about anything yet, and I could already feel B opening up new possibilities.

"Are you going to go wake Ronnie?" B asked with a soft smile.

I needed to work on being present more. "Yes, give me a moment. I'll wake her and change so we can go down to town."

"And I will get us some breakfast for our walk down to Neblig." He headed toward the kitchen.

"Ronnie," I whispered into the dark. "Ronnie, wake up."

She barely even stirred. I went over to the side of the bed and weighed my options: gentle or rough. Easy decision, really.

I rounded her bed and carefully climbed on. I stood and began jumping and hooting, "Ronnie, wake up! It's time to wake, sleepy-head!"

She grunted, and her eyes fluttered open. She glared at me, grabbed the pillow from the other side of the bed, and smacked me in the shins with it, hard. It sent me off balance, careening toward the end of the bed. I stumbled and bounced on the side of the bed before landing on the floor in a crumpled mess.

"Amber?" Ronnie peered over the edge of the bed, concern in her voice. "Are you alright? What were you doing?"

"Waking you up." I groaned. It hadn't been too far of a fall, nowhere near what falling down the mountain would have been, but it still wasn't great.

"And how did you end up on the floor?"

"You don't remember? You hit me with a pillow." I dragged myself up and looked at her.

She laughed in my face. "I was asleep. I just woke up when I heard you hit the floor."

"Ugh. Well, get ready to go into town. B's getting us some breakfast, and I'm going to go change."

"Now? Why?" She turned on the lamp by her bed, illuminating the room, which looked very similar to mine except it was a bit more purple.

"B and I saw a bunch of people gathering in the town square. Don't you want to check it out?" I stood and headed for the door.

"I could have used the extra sleep. I'm jetlagged."

"Getting up and resetting your sleep schedule is good for you." I laughed. "Besides, you slept on the plane and the train, and far longer than I did."

"I can't help it that you're a freak of nature, but some people need sleep."

Even with all her complaining, she got dressed and met B and me in the front hallway. He handed both of us large cheese buns that were still warm and led us down into town. It wasn't the easiest to eat on the way down the mountain, but I managed.

We didn't see anyone as we reached the edge of town. All the hustle and bustle and people leaving their houses that I'd seen from up the mountain had died down. But as we grew closer to the main square, we began to hear the voices of a crowd.

B's pace quickened—he must have noticed them too. The town was eerily empty. Something was happening.

We ran into a wall of people in the square, and I couldn't see a thing. B gasped as he stood tall enough to look over the crowd.

"What is it?" I asked.

B pushed through the group, cutting a path for us. We followed, the crowd closing back in behind us. I was woefully unprepared for the scene in front of me.

Speared on top of the fountain's obelisk-type structure lay a mangled corpse facing up to the sky. Below it scrawled on the fountain in blood was a message in a language I didn't know.

B stared at it, eyes unblinking and tears welling up. I didn't want to bother him, but I had to know what it said.

"Can you read it?" I asked.

He nodded. "It would translate to something along the lines of 'you will not cast us out.'"

"*It's just like Harper all over again.*" Sadness held her face and muffled a sob.

"*It's not like Harper,*" Creativity said, trying to comfort her. "*We don't know anything yet.*"

"*Oh let's be realistic, Creativity,*" Literal said. "*What are the odds that this happens in a place we visit near a festival about driving out evil winter spirits where there are plenty of supernatural creatures in the area? This is no coincidence.*"

"*I never said it was,*" Creativity snapped. "*Harper's wasn't, and neither is this. What we don't know is whether it was from the human contingent of town or the supernatural. With a saying like that, it could be either.*"

"*But who is it?*" Inner Child asked, her voice small.

It looked like it was probably a man, though the body was pretty torn up. Its clothing was in tatters, and I could barely stand to see the sight of the gore.

"Has anyone seen Jetmir?" Bastien called out into the square. He pushed through the crowd and stopped once he saw the body. I looked from Bastien's red face to the mess of a body atop the fountain.

No one responded. No one had seen Jetmir—and everyone had.

Chapter Four

Police buzzed around the body like vultures. An officer took pictures, and they draped a sheet over the body. B tugged on my arm, but I didn't budge. He'd been trying to get me out of the square since Bastien's arrival. I tried not to think about what that might mean. Ms. Avery's kindly face flashed through my mind. I squeezed my mind's eye shut.

"Amber," B hissed. "You don't need to see any of this. Come on, we should go help Bastien. I've never seen those two apart." His voice softened as he looked over to Bastien.

I glanced over to him as well. He knelt in the mud staring up at the words scrawled on the fountain. A strange gurgle came from him, and nothing more. *Did the words mean something more to him?*

Surely if Jetmir had been supernatural in any way, Bastien would know. I'd only seen them once before, but I could tell how close they were from that sole interaction.

I let B pull me along. The crowd watched us join Bastien, and I watched B kneel down in front of him. It just showed how tall a person B was. Bastien looked like a child in front of him.

B whispered things to Bastien that I couldn't hear. Bastien nodded and rose from the mud. B supported him the whole way through the crowd, and once again, Ronnie and I followed as B cut a path for us.

"What are the odds?" Ronnie muttered, more to herself than to me.

"I couldn't even do the math on it. How does one account for being in two highly supernatural places? If it were just pure statistics, that would be one thing, but we both know it's not."

"What?" Ronnie asked as we resurfaced from the crowd.

"You asked what the odds were." We waited in front of the shop as B got Bastien settled inside.

"Oh, right." She shook her head. "Sorry. I guess I must be experiencing what you felt after Harper died. She was a stranger you'd only met once, but you could understand how much people in the town cared about her. It's an odd thing. In a way, everyone is affected by a person dying, but it's different whether you're closer or further away."

I didn't get a chance to respond as B reemerged and said, "We should get back home."

"Why?" I asked.

"Nobody is going to be in their shops right now, and there is no need to go back in there." He nodded toward the crowd and the body beyond.

"What if I don't want to leave?" I asked. I knew it was childish, but I had my reasons for wanting to stay. I needed information. Information that B didn't want me to have, perhaps?

"Amber, don't be difficult." Ronnie gestured for me to come with.

"Fine." I made it clear what I thought of the decision, but I didn't want to make a scene, what with everything else that was already going on. I calmed my hands as they began to shake.

"I'm sorry you had to see that," B said as we climbed up to his house. "I should have gone ahead, I just . . . didn't expect something so awful. Jetmir didn't deserve that." It was a great cover-up. Ms. Avery had cared about Harper too. She'd gone shell-shocked in the aftermath. I couldn't trust a thing he said or did. My mind raced without reason.

"Did you know him well?" Ronnie asked and gave me a pointed look. I guess my face had given my feelings away.

B nodded and I wasn't sure, but I thought I saw the beginning of tears in his eyes. "Better than most, though no one knew him as well as Bastien. Poor Bastien."

"*Oh, he's good.*" Creativity set a mental note. "*If he did this, he's putting on a great show.*"

"*What about Bastien?*" The Originator asked. "*Surely, we should start there. Isn't the closest person usually high up on the suspect list?*"

"*I don't think we can rule anyone out besides ourselves and maybe Ronnie,*" Literal said.

"*Ronnie's only a maybe?*" Inner Child squealed.

"*I mean, I don't really suspect her,*" Literal said. "*I'm just looking at the logic of it all—*"

"*We know.*" Creativity sighed.

"*As I was saying. Logically and statistically, this is unlikely to happen both times we go to a new place. Ronnie is the constant between the two.*"

"*We are also a so-called 'constant.'*" Creativity was spoiling for a fight.

"*Yes, but the difference is we know we didn't do it.*" Literal's tone made it clear she thought Creativity was an idiot.

"Hey. Hey. Hey." Lure tried to get their attention, effectively breaking up the squabbling though that wasn't her design. *"He's staring at us."*

I blinked and sure enough, B was staring at me as Ronnie continued to talk. A shiver ran through me. Did he know I suspected him? How dangerous a being was he? Even if he weren't the murderer, he could have been dangerous. I started to feel that the whole trip might have been a mistake. And how had we gotten inside his house?

I looked down at the tea in my hands. Had B prepared it? I'd been too naive and trusting. I swallowed hard.

"What are you thinking, Amber?" B asked.

So often I wanted people to ask me what I was thinking and they didn't, yet this was a moment where I wanted my thoughts to stay as such. But I had to answer and I couldn't help being honest. "I'm thinking over who might have killed Jetmir. Who is a suspect and why."

"And what have you come to?" B's words were calm and yet I could hear feeling behind them.

"Ronnie couldn't have done it as she was with me nearly the whole time and has no skin in the game. So I can safely rule her out." *How much should I tell him?* "Bastien is obviously high on the suspect list. But I haven't really ruled anyone else out yet."

"Including me?" A bit of a smirk slipped across his face before disappearing just as quickly.

"Including you." I stared into his eyes, willing him to challenge me. Perhaps I was really the one looking for a fight. I clenched my fists so my hands would stop shaking. My body was betraying me.

"And what makes you suspect me?"

Ronnie jumped in. "Is this a good line of dialogue? Let's think this through. It can only end poorly."

But B had already opened the door and I snuck through. "No, he's asked me a question. I'll answer it. You were so very quick to get us out of the square, almost as if you had something to hide. You were against my going back, and you know that I figured out who killed Harper Foster in Coldwater. I'm the last person you'd want learning information about this murder, if indeed you were the murderer."

B nodded. "Now do you want me to tell you why I should think you're a suspect?"

"Go on, then." I couldn't help but laugh at the absurdity.

"Wonderful. This murder only happened after you came to town. This is the second town where you show up and then someone dies. You could have very easily pinned it all on Ms. Avery and now you seek to do the same to me. Why shouldn't I kick you out right now? I have every right. It would be self-preservation."

"You're being irrational. Why would I care to kill someone in a new town? It doesn't make any sense. I have no motive. And to think I thought you were an intelligent person." I felt like a child. I knew I was acting out, but I couldn't stop myself. The words tumbled out faster as I tried to stop them.

"Isn't it all just preposterous?" B's voice grew cold. "Be careful where you throw stones. You might just crack the ice and drown in the freezing water."

Memories of nearly drowning in Coldwater flashed into my mind. He knew about that. I'd told him everything. He'd written so beautifully. I wish I hadn't. At least then he couldn't have thrown it back in my face.

I couldn't even respond. I felt as though I were drowning and B was the one who did it to me.

"Why would I have brought you here right before killing someone when I know you solved the Coldwater case?" he spat.

I lunged up from my seat. If I was going to drown, I'd take him down with me.

"Both of you need to calm down." Ronnie stood up and stepped in between us, facing me. "Amber, you need to come off it. I know you got drawn in last time, but you don't have to do the same here." She gripped my shoulders, but I shook her off.

"Ronnie, this is what I promised to do. There might be creatures out there fighting for their place in this world." I felt my heart sink at the thought. My vision closed in, and I knew I wasn't in control but I didn't know how to stop it, any of it.

Ronnie nodded, "Uh-huh, and you know for a fact one of them is B. So why don't we both calm down and stop accusing each other? It will get us nowhere." She glanced over her shoulder, giving B a look, and pulled me to her. I sank into her arms. For some reason, I felt depleted, like the fight had left me all at once.

"Fine, but next time you ask what I'm thinking, I'll just keep my thoughts to myself." A strange apathy settled over me. I'd relegated my thoughts to the back corner of my mind. "But answer me this: Why didn't you want us to see the body or talk to the police?" My voice sounded flat even to me.

B sighed. "You're from out of town. They never would have talked to you. If anything, your inclination to get involved would have turned you into a target or a suspect." His voice grew small. "I was trying to protect you. Your stories made it clear that you are quite prone to just run right into danger."

I wanted to believe him, but a nagging feeling in the back of my mind told me that it was just an excuse. He was trying to keep me out. It savored too much of my last host and her murderous intent. "I don't believe you."

I could tell he was getting more and more frustrated, but a large part of me really didn't care. "I can go talk to the police later when things have calmed down a little. They know me, and they may want to talk to me anyway since I knew Jetmir. I promise to tell you whatever I find out. Will that suffice?"

"It'll have to do, I suppose." The information would still be filtered through what he wanted me to know, so I'd have to take it with a grain of salt, but he'd be gone for a little while, so perhaps the house would tell me his secrets while he was gone.

"Wonderful, now that that's settled. Why don't we get into some learning? That is the real reason you came here, is it not?" He gave me a pointed look, but I chose not to take the bait.

He led us to a room that smelled of earth and cinders. It was dimly lit with plants growing all around in a tangled jungle. At its center sat a circular hearth with herbs drying around it, and along each wall were counters and hundreds of drawers.

"What is this place?" I gasped and took in the aromas and sight of the room.

"This is a sanctuary. It is where magic is learned, and some magic is practiced." B's voice grew low and monotonous. "Some magic can be done anywhere and, truth be told, much of it was done outside, but through the centuries, these rooms were created for protection. Magic has been castigated and thus relegated to the shadows. But much in the same way that the supernatural is a mere continuation of the natural, magic is a natural art. Some have stronger proclivities toward it, but anyone can pick up on some small aspect of magic.

"From your letters, it seems that Ms. Avery believed that you have more potential than most." He turned to Ronnie. "And you are a supernatural descendant, is that right?"

"Yes, I have at least one supernatural relative, though I believe there are more than one." Ronnie looked at the room with as much awe as I felt.

"You may find it easier to catch on than Ms. Dawson, then." I noted the change. Formality equaled distance. I tried not to let it bother me, but Lure squirmed.

"I also had a bit of training with Ms. Avery. Though I think perhaps your tutelage will far exceed what she would have been able to teach."

"Ms. Avery was one of the best witches I ever met." He furrowed his brow, turning on us. "No matter what she did or thought at the end, she will always be one of the most powerful magic users and best friends I ever had. Is that clear?"

We both nodded.

"Was she supernatural or of supernatural descent?" I asked.

He pretended not to hear me. "Good, now let us get into the fundamentals."

"*Why doesn't he want to answer us?*" The Originator asked.

"*Why didn't we find any idea of what she was in her journals and copious amounts of notes?*" Sadness added.

"*Perhaps she didn't know?*" Inner Child said.

"*But do we really think that B doesn't know what she was? It feels more likely that he's hiding it,*" The Originator said.

"Amber, are you even listening?" B was much closer to my face than I realized. It snapped me back to reality.

"No." I didn't plan on being honest. "No, I decided to not listen to you since you decided to ignore me. It's only fair."

"You do realize that you asked me to teach you, right?" B crossed his arms and glared at me. "You're being childish."

"You're one to talk." I crossed my arms and glared back at him.

He shook his head. "Maybe this was a mistake. I don't need any of this. We'll pick up on this tomorrow, I guess. I have a feeling you're not going to let us accomplish anything until you've gotten the information you want."

He darted out of the room before I could even respond. I moved to follow, but Ronnie grabbed my wrist.

"You've done enough. Truly, I don't know what has gotten into you. It's like you're determined to get us kicked out." She grabbed my shoulders, pulling me toward her when I tried to wriggle away. "This is a great opportunity for us. You need to cool it."

"Ronnie, someone is dead. I have to do something."

I pulled myself from her grasp to go find B. As I entered the hallway I heard the front door slam. By the time I pushed the door open, B's head had disappeared down the mountain.

He'd left me with a golden opportunity. I had full range of his house. I'd either catch him or clear him, and this whole thing would be over.

Chapter Five

I STARTED WITH THE library. If I were going to make someone less suspicious of a place, I would bring them directly to it. I lucked out that Ronnie went back to her room for a nap, though luck was hardly necessary to get her to sleep.

I wasn't sure what I was looking for, but I had a feeling I'd know it if I found it. Besides, everyone had some sort of secret, and he had to have more than one at his age, whatever that age was. Why else would he hold his cards so close to his chest?

I trailed my fingers along the books' spines.

"*Oh, what if he turns into a monster like Beauty and the Beast?*" Inner Child whispered. She was respectful of the library rules.

"*That doesn't make a lot of sense,*" Creativity said. "*The Beast was already a beast, and he was cursed to be like that. B could be a werewolf like Mr. Ward was.*"

"*He doesn't give me werewolf vibes,*" Lure spoke up. "*I could see him as an elf of some kind, or a spirit.*"

"*You think he's a ghost?*" Literal asked.

"No, not a ghost," Lure said. *"More a personification of some sort of natural phenomenon. He does seem a bit obsessed with the idea of the supernatural being the most natural. Trust me, it tracks."*

"She might be onto something," Creativity said. *"Out of the mouths of fools . . ."*

The books didn't tell me much. I didn't have time to go through them all one by one, and most of them were old leather-bound volumes without their titles on their spine. It would have taken too long, and I had to prioritize. I could always come back to the library later. It wouldn't be odd.

I ran my fingers along the wood shelves and pressed my palms to the stone walls. Nothing clicked, pushed, or levered. Whatever B was hiding, it wasn't here.

I went back out into the hallway and headed deeper into what I estimated was the older part of the house. There were only two more doors down that way. The first was on the opposite side of the hall from the library and the other was at the very end, where the hallway actually led. I tried the door across the hall first, but it was locked. I could try and pick the lock, but I still hadn't gotten the hang of it. It was a skill I found particularly difficult to master.

The other door it was. That one opened without an issue. I knew before stepping inside that it was B's bedroom. It smelled like him, like flowers and water. There was a part of me that resisted going in. It felt wrong and invasive.

I heard the patter of small feet at the other end of the hall. *Amethyst!* I didn't think she could see me at the far end of the hallway, but she would soon. It was enough to make me duck inside. I closed the door behind me and waited.

She must have turned off into a different room. I steadied my breath in the darkness before rooting around for the light. It took me a moment and a lot of fur before I landed on the light switch.

I gasped. It was the most gorgeous room I'd ever seen, and it fit B perfectly. The cave walls were a deep blue, and his bed was covered in deer pelts. Most of them were nearly pure white. His comforter was the perfect shade of royal blue to match the dark walls, and everything looked plush and comfortable.

A fire crackled low in the hearth, and a tree grew up around his bed with new foliage and white crystals dangling down from the branches. The chandelier-like strands made the room feel whimsical and icy. The fire warmed it up, reflecting in the crystals and seeming to set the whole room ablaze.

Other than the decorations, the room was simple. Nothing really stood out as particularly B's. It could have very well been another guest room if it didn't feel like B's room in its very character.

I crept around his bed to look at his nightstand, but it was empty. I couldn't even find where he kept his clothes. *Some sleuth I am.*

It all felt like a waste of time. Where did he keep all his secrets? Surely they weren't all in Norway. I was just about to leave when I noticed a door to the left of his bed that was almost completely covered by a curtain.

I scurried across the room and pushed open the door to a study that could have doubled as its own library. This was it. This was where B would unravel. I wasn't sure whether I wanted to clear him or convict him. But I knew I wanted answers.

My stomach growled as I walked around his large desk. He had quite a few shelves of books and below them were filing cabinets. The room was a mess of papers and open books. This seemed to be a place where he spent a lot of time. Perhaps Amethyst wasn't allowed to help him clean it. I could see that as a distinct possibility, though I couldn't fault him for that—I was the same way. Any time Ronnie moved my piles or even a single item, I'd search for it for hours. Chaos was manageable when it was yours alone.

I ducked below the desk as I thought I heard B's bedroom door open and close. He couldn't be home yet—I wasn't ready. I hadn't found a single thing. I waited. I heard movement in his room as he seemed to pace back and forth.

I shifted back up as quietly as I could manage and tried to make sense of his mess. If I moved anything, he'd know. But that was the only way I'd get anywhere. Perhaps he wasn't like me and was just messy.

Then my eye caught on a small letter box. It was ornately carved and in a prominent position where it could be seen from the door and the desk chair. It had to be important to him.

I snatched it and lifted the lid. It slid apart easily, revealing neatly held envelopes with a crisp slit in the top of each of them. I pulled one out and immediately recognized the handwriting for the address. It was mine.

He'd kept every letter pristine in a little box on his desk. It was in plain view in a spot only he would normally be. I didn't know how to feel. This was important, but it wasn't what I was looking for. It was sweet. And it made me the villain.

I ran my fingers over the carvings on the box. They were runes of some kind. I pulled out my phone and snapped a couple of pictures. Perhaps I could use them to identify B.

"*Perhaps they say something about us.*" Lure giggled.

I stifled her the best I could. I had things to do, and I couldn't let feelings get in the way. That hadn't turned out well before.

I closed the box and placed it back on the desk. He'd probably notice if it was moved. The papers strewn across his desk were in multiple different languages. Barely any of it was in English. *I'm getting nowhere.*

I pulled a paper off his desk and in a flash the card box thudded to the floor. B stopped pacing in his room, and there was nowhere for me to go that I wouldn't be seen. I had to make a stand.

I scurried behind the desk and sat in his chair. He stopped in front of the door. I held my breath.

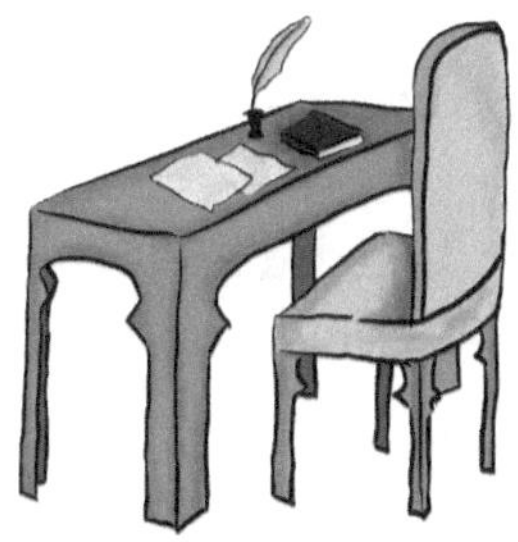

Chapter Six

The door creaked open.

"Amber?" B's face flushed when he saw me and his brow furrowed. "What are you doing in here?"

"I could ask you the same thing." My hands were clammy. How had I gotten here?

"*Let's just tell him we've been infected with brain-eating amoebas,*" Creativity suggested. I ignored her.

"No, you couldn't." B folded his arms. "This is my office, and you have no right to be in here. Not to mention that you had to go through my room to get here." He glanced at the letter box on the floor, and I knew he knew I knew what was in it. It only made him angrier. "What do you think gives you the right to snoop in my room and my study? You accused me and then searched my room. What did I do to deserve this? My friend just died!" He raised his voice at me but was restrained. His voice was crisp, clear, yet reserved and icy. Tears welled up in his eyes.

"You just don't understand." I shook my head and wanted to run.

"What don't I understand?" He towered over me, and I realized just how tall he was. He was dangerous, and I'd just provoked him.

For a moment I was confronting Ms. Avery in her backyard, but this time I didn't feel strong. I didn't feel that conviction of being right.

My breath came fast. I needed a way out. I need my heart rate to go down. The room grew cold, and I shivered; my teeth tried to chatter.

"Why did you bring me here?" My voice came out more forceful than I meant it, but it made me feel more calm. "You're just like her."

"Who?"

"Ms. Avery," I spat. I fought back tears. *Why couldn't I keep control of my body?*

"Is that what this is about?" B softened a little. "Amber, you're being illogical. I brought you here. If I killed Jetmir, I wouldn't have brought you here. What happened with Ms. Avery was different. You went there of your own volition and she had no idea you would be such a good detective. I know you can't let this go. I admire that, truly. I just don't know how I can get you to believe me."

"I'm sorry. Look, I don't want to suspect you." Even as I said it, I knew it was the truth. "It's just . . . it's just . . ." I waved my arms around, unable to come up with the words I wanted to say.

"What is it, Amber? Why am I your villain?" He took a step forward.

I flinched.

He leaned down and picked the letter box up off the floor before he could see my reaction. He looked across the desk as he rose to stand and stopped short.

"What?" His eyes widened in bewilderment. "What did I do? All I did was ask a question."

My lip quivered, and I couldn't stop the torrent of tears that crashed down my face and dripped off my chin. I heaved, and my breath hitched in my throat. Even as my body convulsed, I receded from it.

"*What is going on?*" Literal asked. "*I don't understand.*"

"*This isn't me, so don't you dare give me that look,*" Creativity said, her voice quivering.

"*I'm scared.*" Inner Child clung to The Originator, but it did little good.

"Amber?" B's voice filtered in from a distance. He held me tight in his arms. I should have wanted to flee, but the pressure felt good. Whatever it was was working. "Amber, calm down, it's alright. You're safe. I'm not going to hurt you, I promise." I could hear pain in his voice. He truly didn't want to hurt me. Why couldn't I just believe he was good?

"What's wrong with me?" I choked out. "What's wrong with me!"

He released his arms, and it all came crashing back in, whatever *it* was.

"No," I snapped. "Don't let me go."

He squeezed me tighter again but said, "Amber, I'm not sure what is happening."

"Neither am I." The realization of my own helplessness nearly sent my body into another attack, but his arms held me there. "I'm sorry."

"We're stuck here forever, then." B tried to make a joke but I couldn't quite get myself to laugh.

"If I can get my body to respond to logic." I wanted to get rid of the whole thing as it betrayed me. But slowly my body came back down to some sort of equilibrium and I finally said, "I think you can let me go now."

"Are you sure?" He seemed reluctant, and I thought of the letters.

I nodded.

He set me back down in the desk chair and pulled another chair up to the desk to sit facing me. His voice was soft as he started again. "We still need to talk, but let's both try to be a bit more calm, alright?"

After the liberties I'd taken, he had no reason to be so nice and understanding. I glanced at the letter box and felt guilt gnaw at my stomach.

"We both know you saw it." He looked at me then at the letter box and back to me.

I nodded. "Yes."

"Well?"

"Well, what?"

"What did you think? You saw that I kept every letter you sent in an ornate box. You have to have thoughts about that." He bit the inside of his cheek. Perhaps I was wrong and that bothered him more than my accusations had.

"I don't know what I think. I think lots of things, but it wasn't my place to even know." My body was still trying to be normal.

He laughed. "No, it wasn't, but at least you can tell me what you're thinking about it. That might make it a little more fair."

"Oh, because that went so well the last time." I raised my eyebrows and sat back in the chair. It creaked beneath me.

B sighed. "Look, I understand where you're coming from. It can be hard to trust when it seems everyone around you is living a second life and spinning lies, but I haven't lied to you once. I promise."

"I want to believe you, I really do, but I feel like I can't." I rubbed my hands over my forearms even though I wasn't cold. "It all goes back to Ms. Avery, I think. Maybe I haven't processed it enough, I don't know." My body was still a bit shaky and exhaustion rolled over me. I was depleted.

B nodded and I could see he was weighing something in his mind. He finally made a decision. "Why don't we go back and forth with questions and answer honestly? Does that sound fair?"

"Yes, but can they not be about what I'm thinking? You might not like what you get."

"That is alright by me." He jumped straight in. "Was there a specific reason you came to visit me other than the ones you've already said? I know that Ms. Avery has many contacts, and knowing you, you sent letters to them all upon her death."

I didn't want to disappoint him, but this only worked if we were honest, and I wasn't very good at anything else. "You're right, I did send letters to every contact of hers in her little book. Most didn't reply, though I have a feeling responses will continue to trickle in, as her acquaintances seem secluded like her. Some of the responses were negative or downright nasty. But yours . . . was kind. It stood out to me because you knew the way Ms. Avery had gone and didn't fault her for it." I leaned forward over the desk. "You saw her mistakes and cared about her anyway. At first that scared me a little, but as our letters progressed, I realized my fears were unfounded. However, this murder roused the fears from their slumber." My chest tightened again and it all started to close in.

"Amber?" B noticed it immediately. "Come back to me. I'm not going to hurt you. I'm not Ms. Avery."

I focused on my breath and stared at the papers on the desk in front of me that I couldn't read. It confused my brain enough to shock me out of it.

"Are you alright?" B asked. "Is it alright if I ask another question?"

I nodded.

"What about that scared you?" His voice was soothing, and I imagined he'd changed his question after my episode.

"Ms. Avery did some terrible things." I swallowed but the lump in my throat didn't go away. "I wasn't sure if you were on her side in it, but you never seemed to be. You seem to genuinely care about the supernatural, and not just the more human side of it."

"Hmm, yes, that makes sense." He rested his hands on the desk, close enough for me to touch, but didn't push it. "It's your turn."

"Why did you invite us here? Was it just to teach us, or was it something else?" The question only seemed fair, and I'd have to warm up to the more direct ones.

He grimaced. "Little by little, huh?"

"Little by little."

"Fair enough." He was much more confident than I would have been. "Yes and no. I meant every word that I wrote to you, but my way to honesty is by leaving things out. Omitting things I could not say. Truth be told, your ability to figure out what was going on in Coldwater did seem like a boon. Tensions started to rise at the end of last summer, right before I left to go back to Norway . . ."

"So you brought me here to help you figure out what is really going on in Neblig?" I felt a bit used, but it did make me trust him a little more, which was strange.

"It may have been at the back of my mind, but I really did invite you to learn magic. It just might be more of an even trade than you were bargaining for. I don't know. You seemed competent, and I need help."

I reached out and took his hand. It was cool from being outside. "It's not an even trade. I love mysteries. Why didn't you just say so?" He could be lying but, if he was telling the truth, then he was an unlikely suspect.

"I never got the chance. I guess I planned on us warming to each other a little bit more before throwing you in the deep end, but that wasn't my decision in the end. I'm sorry about how this all came about." He gripped my hand a little tighter. "I didn't realize how bad things were. I wish I hadn't had to leave."

"Why did you have to leave?" I knew it wasn't my turn, but then again it had turned into a conversation, so the turns seemed to matter a whole lot less.

"I always spend half the year here and the other half in Norway. I occasionally go elsewhere, but no matter what, I have to be in Norway from early autumn to late winter." He started to pull his hand away from mine, then seemed to reconsider. "I'm there for the Norse people."

"As what?" I was starting to put it together as his hand didn't grow warmer in mine.

"The wind, the frost, the snow." He hesitated, then squeezed my hands tighter.

I could feel it coming. "What does B stand for?"

"My title." He pursed his lips, as though he didn't want to let the next bit out. He waited for my question.

"So, what is your name?"

"Jack."

My eyes grew wide. "Jack as in Jack Frost? And you spend your spring and summer in the Alps. Do you release your winter powers high up in the Alps where snow never melts?"

He nodded, and there was fear in his eyes. He'd given me something personal, something he maybe shouldn't have told. But I already knew he was supernatural, so why would this be any worse?

"*That's hot.*" Lure blushed.

"*No, it's quite the opposite, actually,*" Literal corrected.

"*Shut up.*" Lure was barely even listening.

"What are you thinking now?" His teeth chattered a little, but it obviously wasn't from cold.

I couldn't tell him what I was actually thinking. "Just processing, that's all. You mentioned your title? I don't remember any myths about Jack Frost having a title. What is it?"

"You're not disturbed or anything? No mob and pitchfork?"

"Did you want me to react like that?" I laughed. "I was stalked by a fish-wolf beast controlled by an evil witch. The fact that you're the personification of winter itself feels simple and calm by comparison. I was dropped in the deep end of this world from the start, but I did my fair share of swimming straight down."

Tension released in his shoulders, and he sat up a little straighter, letting out a sigh. "My title is the North Wind which I inherited centuries ago from my dear friend Boreas. I cannot take his whole name, but I honor him by going by B. Plus, Jack Frost is a name that is too well known."

"What happened to Boreas?" The idea of Jack taking over from him was intriguing.

"He attained freedom." Jack smiled, no doubt thinking of his friend. "He has joined with nature's primal power and become the North Wind as he was always meant to, but someone needed to look after winter and the North. He passed his mantle on to me."

"Thank you for telling me all this. I'm sure it wasn't easy." I took his other hand and looked him straight in the eyes.

He chuckled. "I always planned to tell you, but I thought I'd ease into it more. However, I'm finding that easing into things isn't your style. I'll have to get used to that, but I'm glad I have someone to talk to about this stuff. If it's alright, though, I'd like to leave it there for today."

"Yes, of course." My other questions would just have to wait. I stood to leave, pulling my hands away. The time for vulnerability was over.

"Wait." He stood, blocking my path to the door. "I slid a note under your door on the way to my room earlier."

I glanced at the letter box again. He'd never really answered about that. "Did it have anything to do with those? I guess I never told you what I thought about them or asked you why you kept them in a pretty box."

"This wasn't one of those sort of letters. It was my notes from talking to the police, and I want to apologize if my tone comes across as angry. You have to remember we'd just come off a fight when I wrote it, or were in the middle of a fight." He twisted his long white-blond locks in his fingers. "Though I did mention my intent to work with you, as you are, no doubt, much better at these mystery-solving things than I am." He tried to steer us back on track.

"*Our fight,*" Lure cooed. I didn't let her take the lead.

I chuckled. "I wouldn't be too sure about that. I'm still a novice. Sometimes I think that I figured everything out with Ms. Avery by mere chance."

"I doubt that very much, but even if it is true, this time you won't be working alone. You have Ronnie, and I'll help with whatever I can." He put his hand on my shoulder. I looked into his eyes and instantly knew it was a mistake. I immediately looked away. "I'll take your lead on the mystery, and you can let me teach you magic—sound like a fair trade?"

I pulled back and stuck out my hand. He shook it and didn't let go. "Deal."

"And tomorrow, we can go over what happened at the end of last summer."

"I'll be sure to pick your brain."

He let go of my hand and I left him, heading back to my room where I sat on the bed and wrapped myself up in furs, staring at the fire.

Was I unreliable? I couldn't let what happened with Ms. Avery keep me from being affective, but how could I keep myself from having another episode? I tried to push the thoughts from my mind. I focused on the moment and B.

How had things changed so drastically? He was mad at me, telling me nothing and now . . . now I had a feeling I knew more about B—about Jack—than any other human.

Chapter Seven

My night and day were all mixed up, and I'd fallen asleep staring at the fire. My back ached from slumping down at the foot of my bed. I slid off the end until I lay flat on my back.

Slowly, my muscles relaxed, and I wiggled my back to work out the kinks. My mind came alive. *The papers!*

I searched around me for the papers Jack had slipped under my door the night . . . day before. They weren't in any of my pockets or wrapped up in the furs around me.

I clawed my way back up the side of the bed and found them crumpled in the sheets. I snatched and unfurled them, smoothing them the best that I could. Jack's handwriting was shaky, and I could only imagine what he must have been feeling as the officers told him what had happened to Jetmir. It was succinct and businesslike.

- Between the body's position and the words written beneath it, the police can only believe the worst. There can be nothing suspected other than murder.

- Once the body was removed from the fountain, it was found to be damaged beyond just the chest wound. It is possible the murder was committed by multiple people with multiple weapons.

- The police are unsure as to what killed him. It could have been one of his injuries prior to getting raised on the pike, or it could be the fountain that killed him. They've sent the body to a nearby hospital to see if their forensics teams can get anything off it and to do a more detailed analysis of what weapon or weapons were used and find a clear cause of death.

They confided in me that tensions had been bubbling under the surface since before I left in late summer last year. Truth be told, I was already aware of this fact, and I'm not sure they know the half of it. They have asked me to consult on this case. They know I am well-informed even though I am gone for half the year. However, they may not be clear on the type of information I have and the reason for my having it.

I accepted, with the thought that we might work on it together. However, that is by no means a given and you have every right to refuse.

— B

It seemed Jack did have plans to tell me about the goings-on of Neblig outside of what I'd asked him. It helped his case tremendously, though he could have said that in our initial fight. I tried not to overthink it too much, but that was difficult for me. He had been withholding, and it caused a fight. Perhaps it was just my accusations, perhaps something else.

Then there was the bit about me assisting him. Working with Ronnie was one thing, but working with or under Jack felt different. He knew what I was capable of. He knew what I was doing. It wouldn't be like Coldwater, but then, perhaps nothing ever would.

"*Is Jack in danger?*" Inner Child asked.

"*Why do you think that, dear?*" The Originator asked.

"*The festival is about driving out cruel winter spirits. Jack is a winter spirit.*"

"*I hadn't even thought of that,*" Creativity said, aghast. "*With the words scrawled above Jetmir's body and the festival nearing, there is no way they aren't connected.*"

I showered and got ready for the day, the hot water working out the kinks in my muscles and joints. I checked the weather and was glad to see that it was warmer, but spring in the Alps was much colder than I expected. I ended up wearing a significant amount of layers.

I made my way to the kitchen and met Ronnie in the hallway. "I'm surprised to see you up."

"You're the one who slept through dinner." Ronnie took my arm and walked with me down the hallway.

My stomach growled as if to accentuate her point. "I honestly don't even know what happened. I think there's magic in the fireplace in my room."

She laughed. "Amber, you think there is magic in everything. It was just jetlag."

I didn't argue—I didn't see why it couldn't be a little of both.

We made it to the kitchen, but it was dark. I checked my phone; perhaps we had both woken up in the middle of the night. But my phone said it was 7:45 a.m. I was surprised that Amethyst hadn't already baked up a whole bakery.

"Should we go into town, then?" Ronnie asked after looking into the dark kitchen.

"Sure, we should get to know the place and not rely on Amethyst so much. After all, she didn't ask for us to be here, and we should enjoy the touristy things too. There are so many restaurants to try."

"Ooh, maybe we could walk up to one of the waterfalls. With all the snow melting, they have to be thundering." Ronnie nipped into the kitchen and came out with an apple that she dropped into a pocket in her long flowy pants. "A snack for later—you never know."

I shook my head but let her drag me back toward the front door. If Amethyst or Jack were awake, they didn't show themselves, which was fine by me. I could use a calm morning. With Ronnie, though, that was admittedly an iffy proposition. Maybe I could do a little sleuthing before she dragged me off to a waterfall or four.

"So how are you and B doing?" Ronnie asked as we picked our way down the stone path.

"What do you mean?" It felt weird calling him B when I knew his real name, but I'd wait to see if he told her himself.

"The argument you two got into?" She grinned. "And whatever was going on in his room."

I blushed. "How did you—"

"You weren't exactly sneaky, and he went in after you. It wasn't that hard to put two and two together. So what happened?"

I didn't think she'd put the right two and two together. "Nothing that you're thinking." I didn't know how to talk to her about this without giving it all away. It was Ronnie. I told her everything. We didn't keep secrets.

"Go on." She waved her arms around as we walked into town.

I used the normal bustle of town as an excuse. "I can't talk about it here." I raised my eyebrows suggestively, hopeful she'd understand.

"Oh." Her eyes grew wide. Then she grew serious and drew her hand across her mouth like a zipper and threw away the key. "So where should we get breakfast? I'm starving and I want some cocoa, or maybe some tea."

There was a cute little café with a bear paw print on its sign. People strolled out with steaming cups of coffee, tea, and cocoa.

"The Cozy Cub." I pointed to the sign.

"Since when do you speak Swiss?"

"Swiss isn't a language." I laughed as the doorbell chimed. "They speak German, French, Italian, and Romansch in Switzerland."

"Alright? Which one was that?"

"Swiss-German I believe, but I can't read it. I just remember it from my research." I stepped up to the counter.

"Hello, what can I get for you?" The barista had a thick Swiss-German accent, but she spoke English.

"I'll have your herbal blend." I had to try the Alpine traditional herbal tea. "And a rösti with egg, please."

"I'll have hot cocoa and Kaiserschmarrn." Ronnie stumbled a little but made it through.

"Will that be all today, and is that for here or to go?"

"Yes, for here," I said.

"That will be twenty-two francs."

I pulled out my wallet and paid her. Then we found seats and waited for our food. It didn't take long for them to bring our drinks, and we sat sipping, enjoying each other's company.

"How is the cocoa?" I asked.

"Better than Swiss Miss, that's for sure, and even better than the little stand in the square. It's so thick and rich." She dipped her spoon into the drink, letting it ooze off the end and drip into the cup.

The server brought our food. Powdery pancake bites for Ronnie, and a potato pancake with egg for me. The choices fit us well.

"Is it alright if I work on my story a little bit?" I felt a rude asking, but it was Ronnie. She had all the time in the world to spend with me. If anything, she probably needed a break.

"As long as I can interrupt you without you getting mad." She raised an eyebrow at me.

I gritted my teeth but said, "Fine. I don't think I'll get anything done otherwise."

It took me a moment of staring off into space, notebook in hand for the words to come to me. But I'd learned that rushing them usually didn't work all that well. I read over the last couple of paragraphs and instantly felt connected to Nessi.

Nessi tried to be content with who she was. If Beast liked her, perhaps she should follow his lead and like herself more. But she couldn't stay in one place for too long. Her parents were no doubt still looking for her, but it was more than that . . . she needed to be useful, to find a path forward.

"I know you, Ness." Beast eyed her. "You aren't going to stop until you figure this out, so what's the next step?"

"We never did find humans." She smirked up at him. "I say we do exactly what we planned all along."

"What did the book say?" Beast nestled down beside her and stared into the fire.

"We must pass beyond where dawn and dusk meet."

"Isn't that just the horizon?" Beast asked. "Why do they have to make it sound so mysterious? It shouldn't be hard to reach the horizon."

Nessi laughed. "You think? The horizon is always in front of you. It's impossible to meet the horizon." As she said it, dread flooded over her. It was an impossible task for an impossible creature.

Beast snored beside her. She was still astonished at how quickly he could fall asleep. She stroked his fur and thought she saw something in the fire. It flickered and vanished too quickly to be sure, but it looked like a face that wasn't Petrian or Flourin. It was a face like hers.

And that face whispered words of power.

"Amber," Ronnie tapped me on my arm and I jumped.

"Huh, what?" It took me a moment to focus in on where I was.

"You were mouthing things and moving your shoulders funny. I just . . . well, people were staring." She suppressed a chuckle.

"Oh, sorry. The story was getting intense. I guess I haven't written out in public in a while. My bad." I took another bite of my rösti, which had gone cold. I looked down at my page then back up at Ronnie. "I'm back with Nessi. For some reason, I can't let her go."

"Can I read it?" She gestured for me to hand her my notebook. I hesitated.

"Come on. I've read your stuff before. You're way too hard on yourself. Besides, I'm not really going to understand unless I read for myself. So you might as well hand it over; otherwise, what was the point?"

I reluctantly gave her my notebook and all the while she was reading it, I screamed internally. After a bit, I pulled out a smaller emergency notebook and jotted down some notes for my blog.

There's been a murder. I know, quite the way to start a blog post, but it's true. There are so many questions and I have no answers for myself and even fewer for you. Perhaps I'm bad luck, or maybe I just have it.

On a lighter note, my host has the most endearing home with will-o'-the-wisps in his library that cast everything in blue light. I can't wait to do research and discover more about this town, and now I have the perfect excuse to search even more.

Ronnie finally looked up and said, "It's good." Then she paused before adding, "Have you considered that your writing might be connected to it all?"

"What do you mean?" I put my smaller notebook away.

"Think about your last story with Nessi: you picked a giant wolf as her companion before you knew about Mr. Ward, and if you look at it, Nessi could be finding her way into the human world and discovering it as you uncovered ours." She lowered her voice even though she'd been careful not to mention magic.

"If that's true, what is this story saying?" I didn't disagree with her hypothesis—it was even something I'd considered myself—but I wanted to encourage this line of thought.

"Nothing yet, I don't think. I don't know, maybe we can't see it until we're through it. That's art, right?"

"Maybe, or you're going back and adding meaning where there is none."

"I don't know, prophecy is a power of really strong witches. You shouldn't just brush it off." She popped up out of her chair and made for the door.

I scarfed down the last bit of my rösti and tea and followed her.

Once we were outside I asked, "Do you really think I might be a naturally gifted witch of some kind?"

She stopped in the middle of the road and turned to me saying, "Amber, there is no doubt in my mind that you are something extraordinarily special. Who knows, perhaps your books are the way you prophesy. I've seen people prophesy with art and music.

It does seem to often come out of creative pursuits. Now come on. Those waterfalls aren't going to fall forever."

I laughed and followed her toward the trail. "I think that is exactly what they do."

As we left town, I noticed a couple people giving us weird looks. I couldn't quite figure out why. Perhaps they didn't like newcomers. It was a strange thought, however, since tourism was so vital to this town's livelihood.

I also noticed that Bastien wasn't sitting in his customary rocking chair. One thing was clear: Jetmir's death had hit Neblig hard, and Jack was right—there was something strange, an undercurrent of tension I hadn't noticed before.

Ronnie and I both glanced at the fountain in the center of town, and it looked to have been washed clean. There were also notably a few more decorations for the coming festival. Perhaps more people were worried about evil spirits than usual, and could anyone blame them? On the other hand, maybe this was by design. To that end, why would someone want those in Neblig to be afraid? If I figured out the answer to that, the whole thing might unravel.

Chapter Eight

RONNIE BOUNCED A LITTLE as we approached the first waterfall. We could see it even from a distance and hear it anywhere in Neblig, but nothing prepared me for standing right in front of it.

"Isn't it beautiful?" Ronnie gasped. "Oh, and look at the sheep just grazing all happy. It must be calming."

The thundering water nearly drowned out her voice completely. I had to strain myself to hear her. Soon we got close enough to the falls that, though she kept talking, I couldn't hear her at all.

The waterfall was like nothing I'd ever seen before. The plummeting water drenched nearby rocks to create huge dripping icicles, which over time formed tubes of ice with water pouring out the center.

"How many Undine do you think are a part of this waterfall?" The Originator asked.

"Seven!" Inner Child screamed. *"At least seven."*

"Is there a calculation?" Literal asked. *"A certain amount of water per Undine?"*

"That's the dumbest thing I've ever heard," Creativity scoffed. *"There is no exact amount. It has to do with the spirit of the water and its flow."*

"Is anyone else wondering what Jack is doing right now?" Lure asked, unknowingly providing the perfect buffer between Literal and Creativity. *"No,"* The Originator said. *"Did you have something else to add, Lure?"*

"Not about the waterfall. Could you be any more boring?"

Ronnie grabbed my hand and pulled me down the path until I could hear her again. "What's going on with you and B?"

"What?" I hated how well she'd grown to read me. "Whatever gave you that idea?"

"You had that look. The same look you had after Logan pulled you from the Hudson. So spill, is there something going on with you two?"

"How do you know that my face had anything to do with him?" I shoved Lure deep, deep down. "I'm nowhere near him."

"Amber, he's the only man you've really interacted with in any meaningful way since coming to Neblig. Unless you want to tell me something about Bastien. I mean, I did notice you looking at his store. Perhaps it was longing in your eyes." She was messing with me.

"Knock it off."

"So are you romantically inclined toward B?" She didn't even know his real name, but I did.

"I shouldn't be."

She smirked. "I didn't ask if you should or shouldn't be. I asked if you are or aren't."

"I don't know yet, okay? And I really don't want to talk about it. If and when I figure it out, you'll be the first one I tell. You know that."

Ronnie crossed her arms but didn't push any further. It seemed that for the moment she was satisfied, but who knew how long that would last.

We saw two other waterfalls on that side of the valley; neither of them was as grand or thundering as the first one, but there was something about the slower waterfall with its trickle around and through the rocks that stuck with me. It separated and then rejoined itself, going by many paths and yet coming back together in a pool at the end.

"Should we get back?" Ronnie asked, looking up at the midday sun.

"Probably not a bad idea. I have a mind to explore town more." We started back.

"You just want to investigate, don't you?" Ronnie laughed. "So predictable."

"I'm really starting to think we need a break from each other. You know me too well."

Ronnie stuck out a quivering lip. "I'm hurt. I really am." She could be so dramatic when she wanted to.

I laughed at her and stopped in front of the fountain. They'd done a good job cleaning it. I wouldn't get much off it in the way of clues, but I couldn't help but wonder if this was actually where Jetmir had died.

"Do you think we should be standing here?" Ronnie asked.

I didn't take my eyes off the fountain, as if looking away would change it somehow. "*You will not cast us out.* That's what B said the sign translated to. If we believe he was telling the truth, what does that mean?"

"He was," a voice said from behind us. I vaguely recognized it and turned.

The tall, well-dressed man from Aelyn and Nisse's house stood between us and Bastien's store. His eyes looked sad, but they were sharp too. We'd barely gotten to know B's friends, and perhaps that was a good place to start.

"Branson, right?" I asked.

"That's right, the one and only. I'm sorry you're here under such sorrowful circumstances. It really is poor timing." He shook his head and shoved his hand in his pocket, fiddling with something.

"We're sorry for your loss," Ronnie said, joining the conversation.

"Did you know Jetmir well?" I was having trouble getting a read on the man. He was organized and neat, but his face was expressionless.

"We were friends." He nodded. "I just came from talking to Bastien. He's not doing so well, very volatile. I had to step outside. Can't blame him though."

"Where are you off to now?" Ronnie asked.

"Aelyn and Nisse's. They invited me for breakfast. All of us need a little extra company right now. Is B coming down anytime soon? I know he's not the most social but . . ." He trailed off then said, "Anyway, I should get going. I thrive on punctuality." He sped off without another word or waiting for an answer to his question.

"That was odd," I watched him disappear among the houses.

"Grief does strange things to people."

"So does guilt." I squinted, trying to keep an eye on him, but he was gone.

"We're going to talk to Bastien, aren't we?" Ronnie stated more than asked.

I nodded and clomped up the stairs to the front door. We had a murder to solve, no matter how uncomfortable it might get. With a deep breath, I stepped inside.

Bastien grumbled to himself as the bell on the door chimed. He looked up with brow furrowed and mouth pursed, but softened when he saw it was Ronnie and me. He took a moment to reset himself.

"Hello, what can I do for the two of you?" He did his best to sound cheery, but it was a thin veneer. I could imagine he just wanted a bit of normalcy. That was something I could understand well.

"We never really got to visit the other day," Ronnie began.

I saw no reason to be fake. "Plus, we were in town and wanted to see how you were doing." It was an easy answer: he wasn't doing well. But I had to wonder about his interaction with Branson. Bastien seemed perfectly calm now, but when we'd first come, he'd nearly yelled at us. What had Branson said or done? I tucked the thought away for later dissection.

"Is it alright if we don't talk about it? I've had enough people ask me how I'm doing that I'm ready to close up shop and cast myself into one of the waterfalls." He sighed. "I just want people to come shopping like usual."

"Noted." I said and began browsing through his store. It was an odd collection of things. There were normal wares that most grocery stores would have, but there was also climbing gear and a small collection of handmade sweaters, some embroidered artwork in simple frames, and packets of herbs that the average person would have no use for.

"*Branson and Bastien must have had a fight,*" Literal said. "*It's the only thing that makes sense.*"

"*Do you think it has something to do with the unrest that Jack mentioned?*" Creativity asked. "*Or is it just friends having a disagreement about the death of a mutual friend?*"

"*Bastien seems on edge,*" The Originator added. "*Either could be true.*"

"*Can we get some candy? Those green ones look tasty. I wonder if they're sour.*" Inner Child took over, pushing thoughts of mystery out of my mind.

I grabbed a pack of the green candies and a shopping basket. Ronnie's basket was already mostly full. I tossed a couple more items in, including a cute blue and white sweater, and then joined Ronnie up at the counter.

"I'm sorry about earlier," Bastien said as he processed Ronnie's purchase.

"No need to apologize," Ronnie said. "I understand a bit too much what you must be going through." Her voice broke a little, and Bastien looked at her with tears in his eyes.

"Did you lose someone?" He was struggling to keep it together.

Ronnie nodded. "Two people, actually."

"How long have they been gone?" He stopped processing our purchases and gave Ronnie his undivided attention.

"About six months, and I still miss them every day." Ronnie fidgeted with one of the bracelets she wore, and I reached out to take her hand.

"Who were they to you?" The conversation seemed to be making him feel better. This wasn't something I could have done. Ronnie had a knack with people.

"My aunt and a really good friend." Ronnie's voice caught, and I squeezed her hand. "And Jetmir?"

"Good friends, business partners, and my half brother." He started scanning items again as if he needed something to do to be able to talk. "He was the last family I had. Now it's just me, alone in the world." I could see how unmoored he felt.

"Was there any indication that he had problems with anyone?" I asked. Ronnie was good at relating, but she wasn't always the best at asking the right questions. That was my thing.

Bastien took a moment to focus on me almost as if he'd forgotten I was even there. "Um, not really. Jetmir got along with everyone well. He had a certain way about him that made it easy for him to make friends." I thought of Ronnie, and that brought up the idea of her dying and what I would do if that happened. I did my best to push the thought out of my mind.

"He didn't have any sort of argument in the days leading up to . . ." I didn't want to say it. It could trigger him and then we'd lose all our progress.

"No, not that I'm aware of. If he had issues with anyone, he didn't tell me about it. I don't know why he wouldn't." He glanced over at an apron hanging on the wall, a J embroidered on it. "Though he had been acting a little strange. I could tell something was bothering him, but he didn't share with me and I didn't push. He just needed time to get his thoughts sorted before sharing them, like he always did. Only this time . . ."

". . . this time he didn't have the chance," Ronnie finished his sentence.

Bastien looked up, eyes red. "I should have asked him."

"Don't do that to yourself." Ronnie reached across the counter and grabbed his hand. "You had no way of knowing. I know you want someone to blame, but you can't blame yourself. I promise we will find out who did this. Trust us."

"What about Branson?" I asked. "Why were you going to yell at him when we came in?"

"How did you—"

"She's good at this." Ronnie smiled at him. "She's a freak of nature."

"Thanks." I put my hand on my hip.

"Branson just doesn't get it, that's all." Bastien shook his head, tears flying off onto the counter. "I shouldn't expect him to, but I thought he cared for Jetmir. No one cared for Jetmir more than I did. I'm sorry, but I don't really want to talk anymore." He rushed through the rest of our items and hurried us through our transaction. "Have a nice day," he called to us as we headed out.

Once on the front steps I said, "That went better than I thought it would."

"I think he's hiding something," Ronnie said.

"What makes you say that?"

"He doesn't want to talk about the conversation with Branson. You brought it up twice, and he avoided it both times. There's something there."

I didn't disagree, but I figured one of us needed to play devil's advocate. "Maybe it was just a sensitive moment for Bastien, and Branson just pushed too hard."

"It's possible," she said as we headed back toward Jack's side of town. I dreaded climbing up the mountain with groceries. "But I would think you'd know one way or another."

"I do, I just—"

Neblig disappeared for a moment as I stood in front of a stone wall with budding ivy growing up it. Then I was back.

"You disappeared again." Ronnie laughed a little, but I could hear concern behind it and this time, I wasn't sure if I'd actually disappeared or not.

Before I could respond I saw Jack strolling toward us. He wore only a thin white cotton shirt with light blue patterned stitching, and some light slacks. Now that I knew who he was, it was so obvious. I couldn't believe I hadn't put it together myself, but I had more pressing things on my mind—like where had I just gone?

"How's Bastien?" Jack asked, looking at our bulging paper bags.

"As good as can be expected." I glanced around the street to make sure we were alone. "He had a disagreement with Branson before we came in, though. Do you know much about their relationship?"

"Jetmir and Branson were friends more than Bastien and Branson ever were." Jack shook his head. "I don't know. I've seen grief presented in many different ways throughout my time. Though it could be something more, something to do with the unrest. Where did Branson go? Is he still at Bastien and Jetmir's shop?"

My time. I hadn't given much thought to Jack's age and what that meant for me, for any potential us. Centuries or millennia were sure to do strange things to someone's idea of relationships. I couldn't think about that. It was a distraction.

"He said he was going to Aelyn and Nisse's," Ronnie replied when I didn't.

"We should go there, then." Jack reached over to me and took my paper bag. "Let me take that."

I didn't protest. We walked back through the center of town, and I wondered at how many times we'd passed the fountain.

"*Whoever did this wanted it to be known and remembered. No one that saw that display could forget it when they traverse through the heart of Neblig,*" Sadness droned.

"*Which means that whoever did this had some other motive.*" Literal smiled, which was in stark contrast to Sadness. "*If we can determine a motive for each suspect then all the pieces will fall together.*"

"*Yes, that is how solving a mystery works,*" Creativity scoffed.

I barely even noticed Neblig disappear from view this time as I was so wrapped up in my thoughts. The ivy-covered wall rose up in front of me once more, and I smelled warm dirt. I turned around, and there at my feet was a single red poppy. It looked like a drop of blood. Fear coursed through me, and I ran from it. Deep in my bones, I knew there was something wrong about this place.

Chapter Nine

MY BODY ACHED AS if I'd just run a marathon—or at least that's what I thought it felt like, as I'd never run a marathon. Everything hurt, not least among them my head. Though that was nothing compared to the emotional weight that rested in my chest and the smell of dirt and decay in my nose. In other words, I was a mess and I had no idea where I was.

"Amber?" Ronnie said from nearby.

My eyes fluttered open and I looked up at a room full of people, which is not what I wanted to see. Ronnie and Jack were there, and so were Aelyn, Nisse, and Branson.

"What happened?" I mumbled, though my tongue felt heavy and thick.

"Do you have a history of seizures in your family?" Nisse asked.

I tried to shake my head but it hurt so I said, "No, not that I'm aware of."

"You stopped and just stared at the fountain for a while," Jack said. "At first we thought you were merely thinking, but it went on for a little while. Ronnie waved her hand in front of your eyes and you didn't notice. Then I picked you up and carried you here."

"How long was I unresponsive?" The aches had dulled a little bit, and I wondered where they'd come from. From what Jack said, I hadn't fallen, so I shouldn't have been injured.

"A few minutes at most," Aelyn said. "The fountain isn't that far, and B moved fast. He'd only just laid you down when you started to come back to us, dear."

I glanced down at the bed and took in the room behind the people, for the first time. It was a small guest room with a single bed and paintings of waterfalls and nature on every wall. The water imagery was calming, as if hung specifically for this situation.

"Can you give us a minute alone?" Jack asked the other three. "I hate to impose and kick you out of your own guest room, but maybe Amber would feel more comfortable if there weren't quite so many people standing around."

Thankfully, they agreed and left me with just Jack and Ronnie. Aelyn ran off to the kitchen to tend to whatever had started to smell like it was burning, and after a moment I could hear Nisse and Branson talking low in the living room.

"What did you just experience?" Jack asked once the room was clear. It was almost as if he knew there was something else going on.

"It wasn't the first time. Ronnie can attest I had a moment right before we met up with you, but I guess this one was a bit . . . longer." I bit my lip and then said. "I saw something. It doesn't make much sense to me, but the first time I saw an ivy-covered wall; I blinked and it was gone. When it happened again in the square, I saw the wall and turned around to see a poppy at my feet. Then I ran."

"Why did you run?" Jack's eyes blazed with intensity.

"I was scared. I don't know what of, but I was scared." I could still feel it as I lay on the bed looking up at him.

"I'm going to have to worry every time you stop to think now, aren't I?" Ronnie sighed.

"I hope not." I wasn't sure what to think about it all. What if I continued having episodes?

"What if it's a premonition?" Ronnie's eyes flashed as the idea hit her. "Maybe writing your story brought on some sort of premonition."

"Why would that have just started now?" It wasn't the worst theory, and I had nothing to base it on, so she could have been right.

"I don't know. Magic is strange." Ronnie shrugged.

"We should run some tests." Jack paced back and forth as he seemed to weigh something in his head. "Do you think you have it in you to climb up the mountain? We need to go somewhere. I'll explain when we get there."

I fought the urge to object—and after a brief internal struggle, I simply nodded. It was time for me to stop firing aimless accusations at every helpful suggestion offered me.

He smiled as if acknowledging my mental efforts. "It's easier to explain if you see it. Trust me."

A light knock came at the door, and a moment later Nisse popped his head in. "Is she doing any better?"

"Yes, I'm not aching much at all anymore." I realized after I said it that I'd never mentioned my aching before.

"Wonderful, if you can make it out to the dining room, we would love to give you some tea and cookies." Nisse was such a gentle sort of man. "She only burned a couple of them."

"We'll be out in a moment; thank you for your hospitality." I was truly grateful. This was hardly the sort of thing I wanted to happen in the center of town, especially when people were already on edge. I turned back to Jack and asked. "What kind of unrest was happening before you left last autumn?"

"What? Are you really asking about that now? It's hardly pressing." Jack leaned back from me.

"It's the perfect time to get information." I propped myself up and leaned on the wall for support. "They won't suspect that I'm being anything other than interested right now as I've just had an episode and I needed to interview them anyway so why don't we kill two birds with one stone."

"And get some cookies out of it," Ronnie added.

"B, I need more information if I'm going to investigate this." I rotated my ankles this way and that. "Tell me about the end of last summer and whatever place it is you feel is necessary to take us."

Jack turned, eyeing the door—the other three were talking in the dining room. He sighed. "There were break-ins and strange occurrences. None of it was proven to be magic. They were the kind of things that could just be freak effects of nature like a massive infestation of frogs or a mud slide, but combined with the break-ins it became strange. On top of this, another town was involved, higher up in the mountains. That's where I was going to take you to see about this episode you just had. Both places had issues, but there were more break-ins and odd goings-on of a 'normal' nature in that town and more magical ones going on here in Neblig."

"Are there more magical creatures that live in the other town?" I was fairly certain I already knew the answer.

"Yes, more magical creatures live there."

"So we need to investigate them too. We'll discuss this more after tea and cookies. Let's go talk to your friends before they come back in search of us, then." I shifted, preparing to stand.

Jack reached over to help but I turned away, putting all my weight on my feet. As soon as I did, I stumbled, and my vision went funny. Jack grabbed hold of my arm, steadying me. I shivered.

"Are you alright?" Jack's concern was evident.

I looked at Ronnie across the room and her smirking face made my stomach churn. I wasn't ready for any of this. Why couldn't Jack be the old, very much not-attractive man I'd imagined when writing those letters?

I pulled myself away from him and headed toward the door without reply. It wasn't far to the dining room, which I was grateful for as I didn't fancy Jack having to carry me again. Getting aid from him felt far too much like Logan saving me from the Hudson. I didn't want to think about Logan.

"It's about time," Aelyn said as I stumbled into the room. "Are you feeling better, dear?"

"Yes, thank you for opening up your home to us." I smiled but winced as I felt a twinge in my side.

"Any friend of B's is a friend of ours. Sit. Sit." She ushered me around the dining table to a chair across from Branson and Ronnie, then took the seat beside me. Jack sat across from her, and Aelyn and Nisse took the head and foot of the table, though which was which I wasn't sure. "Tell us—what do you think of Switzerland so far?"

Ronnie chuckled and took the question, which gave me time to think. "Well, we haven't seen much of it yet, but I for one am very impressed. It's so picturesque."

"How did you all meet?" Nisse asked as he munched on a gooey cookie. "B doesn't tell us much. He likes to keep his distance." I noted tension between the two of them; perhaps Nisse felt that Jack wasn't really a part of their group.

"It's not the best of stories," I started. "We had a mutual friend who passed, and when we went through her estate, I took it upon myself to reach out to her far-flung friends across the globe. Her husband's work had taken her all over the world."

"And I knew her from one such trip to Norway," Jack added. "I was glad to hear news of her, even though it was the worst kind, so

I wrote back, and we continued sending letters until we decided to meet in person."

Nisse nodded, his mouth full of cookie. Aelyn bounced up out of her chair and scampered off to the kitchen again as if she couldn't stay still. Only Branson was fully engaged in what Jack was saying.

"Are we not going to talk about the elephant in the room?" Branson finally said. "We're acting as though someone didn't die here yesterday. All condolences for your friend, but we just lost someone." His face scrunched up, and at first I couldn't tell whether it was anger or tears that he held back. Or both.

Jack nodded and spoke soft and low. "What did you want to say about it, Branson?"

"The fountain." I could tell he was seeing it in his mind: Jetmir impaled on the spire. "Why did they choose the fountain? Why would someone kill Jetmir, of all people? It just doesn't make sense. Are we safe?" He glanced between Ronnie and me.

"They are safe, if that is what you're wondering," Jack reassured him.

"Someone's trying to drive us out!" Branson exploded. "They've already gotten rid of most of us, and now they want the rest gone."

I looked at Jack. "What is he talking about?"

Jack sighed. "Neblig used to be more open to magical and supernatural beings, like most of the world was, but there was a purging of the . . . more noticeable magical creatures. The only ones who can come into Neblig are those of us who can blend in. Those in this room."

"The place in the mountain, that's where magical creatures ran to?" It made perfect sense, and it broke my heart.

Jack nodded.

"We have to go there, then. Maybe they can help us figure out who killed Jetmir."

Branson shook his head. "Why would they know? It was a human who killed him, no doubt. He must have figured out Jetmir was one of us and killed him for it.""Then we're all in danger." Jack furrowed his brow. "All the same, we will go there and make sure everything is alright." He purposefully didn't mention my ailment. "Besides, I have to check the integrity of my enchantments."

"Very well, I was planning to make the trip today anyway." Branson reached into his pocket and fidgeted with something. "In fact, I should go now. I have a meeting and I'm going to be late." He got up and called into the kitchen. "Thank you for having me over again, Aelyn." He turned to Nisse. "Thank you, Nisse. And it was nice getting to know you two." Then he hopped out of the house as if he were glad to be rid of us.

"Does anyone else think he's being strange?" I asked.

Nisse laughed. "Branson is always a bit strange. As long as I've known him, he's been a nervous sort and I know Jetmir's death is weighing heavy on him. It weighs on us all."

"Thank you for everything, Nisse," Jack said. "I think we'll take our leave too, as long as Amber is feeling well enough for the trip up the mountain."

"Yes, I'm feeling much better." It wasn't a complete lie. I had indeed mostly recovered, but perhaps not enough to scale a mountain. "May I take a cookie with me?"

Nisse pushed the plate toward me. "Take as many as you'd like."

Ronnie took him up on that as if it were a challenge, and by the time we stepped outside her pockets were bursting and she smelled of sugar and chocolate.

"That was interesting." Ronnie munched on some cookies. I felt like she and Nisse would get along well. "Branson's an antsy one."

"Yes." Jack rubbed his chin. "That whole interaction was strange, but you can see them reacting to their grief differently. Aelyn wants to provide, and Nisse is eating his feelings. Branson is . . . doing whatever that was. Come on, we should get going if we intend to have time to investigate."

I was grateful for the silence as we climbed up to his house. The exertion actually seemed to soothe my aches and grounded me a little bit more.

"How are you holding up?" Jack asked me, flashing an icy smile.

"I've been better, but I think it'll pass." I swallowed. "We should drop the groceries inside and continue on before I lose my gumption altogether."

"Oh, please tell me we can at least get some food first," said Ronnie. "If I'm climbing farther up a mountain, I need fuel." She panted, playing it up for effect. I tried to ignore her bulging, cookie-filled pockets.

Jack chuckled. "Of course, go in and grab something quick. But we must leave soon, as I don't want to be out too long after dark. Did you know there are lynxes and bears about? Bears that have only just come out of hibernation. I imagine they are quite hungry."

"Bring me something!" I called after Ronnie. I may not be quite so hungry but I imagined I might get there after some exertion.

"Jack?" I said, once she was gone. My heart pounded. *What was I going to say after his name?*

He pulled his attention from whatever he'd been looking at in the far mountains. For a moment I wondered if he could see that far. "Yes, Amber?"

My hands grew sweaty. "Ronnie saw me go into your room and then she saw you do the same." My throat went dry, making it hard to get words out. "What I mean is, she knows we talked and I have to give her something. She's already assuming . . ."

"You want me to tell her who I am?" He didn't seem upset by the thought.

"*If only we could see inside his head,*" Literal said.

"*Or . . .*" Lure tried to say.

"*Nope. Just nope.*" Literal would have blushed if she could.

Even with Literal's intervention, I had to work extra hard to continue looking at his face.

"I think it will come out one way or another, and it's probably better coming from you. At least that way she won't feel bad about knowing it. Then we can all talk freely. She's a part of this too. It's not just the two of us."

He paused for a long moment and then said, "Yes, I guess so. Since you decided to bring her along."

"What is that supposed to mean?" Heat burst to life in my chest from more than just exertion. I didn't like the implication that Ronnie was a tagalong, or unwanted.

"Oh, I'm sorry. I didn't mean anything by it." He put his hand on my shoulder. "Ronnie is more than welcome, and I'm happy to have her here. I'm just saying that I know you were considering coming on your own at first. That's all."

The front door opened, and Ronnie came out, juggling more than two sandwiches. She had a backpack on, but it looked as though she hadn't filled it at all. Jack was lucky for her interruption, but it left me to stew.

Jack pulled his hand from my shoulder as if he'd been caught, but Ronnie wasn't paying attention to us. She was focused on not dropping anything. I rushed over to her and started taking things out of her hands.

"What is all this?" I asked as she loaded up my arms with meats and cheese, a whole loaf of bread, and quite a bit of fruit.

"Amethyst wasn't happy about something. She practically threw all these things at me and told me to get out." Ronnie looked up at Jack. "Did something happen between you two? Because I don't think the verbal battering I just received was my fault."

"No," Jack said, helping with the food. "She doesn't like sudden changes in plan, and I didn't tell her about this trip. Maybe that upset her. I always meant to bring you both in on the magic of

Neblig and its surroundings, but everything has gotten so strange so fast. It's ruined Amethyst's cooking plans, I'm sure."

"I see. Well, I guess we're having a little picnic." Ronnie had already cut off a chunk of cheese now that her hands were empty and mine were full. "Come on, that big rock will do nicely." She pointed to the big flat rock overlooking Neblig that I'd sat on the other day.

We ate a quick lunch, and I was glad to get off my feet for a bit, even knowing it would be harder to start again after resting. The meat and cheese hit the spot, and I didn't even take the time to turn it into a sandwich. I just nibbled on a bit of everything until I got all the desired flavors.

Once we were done, we packed everything into Ronnie's backpack. Neither of us knew how far we were going, so it was better to be on the safe side should we get a bit peckish.

"I'll take that." Jack reached out for the pack.

Ronnie didn't give it to him.

"Come on," Jack waved for her to give it to him. "We have a ways to go and I've trekked this way countless times, but it may not be so easy for you two. Let me be considerate and helpful."

Ronnie reluctantly gave him her bag, but not before pocketing a few things from it. I couldn't quite get a good glimpse of what she'd felt necessary to keep on her.

"How long a journey is it?" I asked.

"It usually takes me an hour and a half, so for us—probably closer to two hours." He led us around the side of his house to a small trail that led farther up into the mountains.

"You think we'll slow you down by a third?" Ronnie asked.

"It seems like a proper estimate, yes." Jack was unfazed. I don't think he even realized that what he said might be offensive.

We trekked off up the mountain without knowing exactly where we were going. I was about to ask for more information, but Jack beat me to it.

"I'm not always the best at talking," Jack began. "I believe it's because language has evolved so much and keeping the current terminology in my mind is extraordinarily difficult, but Ronnie, I have something to tell you. Amber already knows, but as you are two peas in a pod, it is important that you know too." He gave me a little nod, which I took as an apology for earlier.

Ronnie puffed out, "What is it, B?"

"I'm Jack Frost." And just as if he'd conjured them up, snowflakes began falling around us. "You know I do work up North during the winter, but the work I do up North *is* winter, and I spend my spring and summer here where I can release my powers up into the highest peaks. No one notices because the snow never melts."

"Well, that's interesting, Jack. What happens if you don't expel your magic?" Ronnie yelled over the whipping wind. It tried its best to pull her voice down into the valley below.

"Discomfort at first, then pain everywhere as my body tries to rip itself apart, and if I don't expel it at that point, I dissolve back into nature. My very being will consume me. It's what my predecessor Boreas did. I've taken on his mantle, but I think it only hurts if you fight it. What he did was a little different, where he gave into it completely."

"Have you ever come close to letting go?" I asked. "It must be tempting after so many centuries of existence. Don't you get tired?"

"I'm always tired. But it is my normal." He sighed. "There was a time when I barely even existed. The only thing that called me back was that there was no one to replace me; no one would care for me after I was gone as I do for Boreas. That was something I couldn't bear."

He fell silent as we trudged on. The air grew thinner, and I was having trouble keeping Jack's pace. It was clear that Jack's estimate had been overly generous. Neither Ronnie nor I were used to such high elevation. Snow flurried around us, but I felt warm. I wasn't sure if it was from the exertion or if Jack was somehow protecting us.

We cleared a ridge and looked down into a great crater of snow and sharp ice. I looked over at Jack, and he was smiling.

"We're here." His smile looked sinister.

Was I right all along? Had he brought us here to kill us, and used the magical creatures living peacefully in the mountains as a ruse? Cast us down on one of the sharp spikes and spear our bodies, painting the snow red?

"Where is here?" Ronnie asked. "This is a crater of snow. This was your grand reveal? What gives?"

"Oh, sorry. I forgot you couldn't see." Jack snapped his fingers.

The whole crater transformed in front of our eyes. The fragrant aroma of flowers rose to meet us, and a town appeared as if it had always been there—and perhaps it had. In the heart of winter was . . . spring.

Chapter Ten

I shucked off a couple of layers of clothes. The small valley was wild and warm, lush and filled with life. Even after months of seeing fantastical creatures in day-to-day life, the town was hard to believe. But stranger still was seeing wild animals in pastures, like deer, ibexes, and mouflon as if it were a normal everyday occurrence.

"What is this place?" I twirled around in the field of flowers on the outskirts of town, and I felt whole in a way that I hadn't felt since childhood.

"A small paradise." Jack smiled, but it wasn't sinister at all. I felt bad for ever thinking it.

"*What if it's a trap?*" Creativity asked. "*The most dangerous predators lull their victims into a false sense of security. Isn't this exactly what we'd need to let our guard down? Jack would know that.*"

"*Dandelions,*" Inner Child squealed.

I dashed into the flowers and came up with a bouquet.

"Amber, be careful," Jack said, taking my other hand. "Not all of the residents would take kindly to you rooting around and stealing."

". . . I don't know what came over me, sorry." I dropped the flowers.

He picked up the flowers and tucked them into Ronnie's back-pack, which he still wore. "Welcome to Silvaruin. It's a haven for creatures and magic. There are more of these places than you'd think, but fewer than there should be. Come, let me show you around."

He led us through the fields of flowers into town. The buildings were constructed much the same as the ones in Neblig, but they were more colorful. In fact, they matched the colors of the field of flowers and gave a childlike, cotton candy sort of feel.

"Jack?" I asked, getting his attention. "Why is it already fully spring here? There is snow just up the ridge and yet it doesn't touch the town."

"Silvaruin needs to be protected, and that means we can't have hikers finding it, or satellites as is now a problem." He led us toward the center of town. "So I do my best to keep the town hidden. The snow is an illusion, but it is still cold. If you had a tall enough ladder, you could probably peek your head through and see above it. Think of it as snow clouds."

"But we can see the sky." I was having a difficult time wrapping my head around it.

"Think of it as a very cold one-way mirror. We can see out, but others can't see in. Even with thermal imaging it looks cold."

It was at this moment I realized we hadn't seen any creatures other than the animals in the pastures and stables. The town seemed eerily deserted. I was just about to ask Jack about it when he let out a strange call.

All at once, the town burst to life. Doors opened, windows un-shuttered, and creatures came out of the woodwork, some of them quite literally. I took a step back. My flight instinct was triggered by the sudden movement.

"Jack!" A cry went up from all around, and the townsfolk crowded in around us.

There were dryads, satyrs, some human-looking beings, goblins, kobolds like Amethyst, and plenty of creatures that I couldn't immediately identify. Fear and excitement joined in my heart.

"Back up, now. I don't want you scaring our guests," Jack said, but he wasn't speaking English. He wasn't speaking any language I knew of, and yet I understood it. I had to strain, but I could clearly understand his meaning.

When the crowd receded and gave us some much-needed breathing room, I was left wondering if I could speak this mysterious language as well as understand it.

"Sorry, they're just very excited," Jack said to us in English. "I don't bring people to the valley often. In fact, I don't bring people here ever." He blushed. I don't know if I was just reading into things or if he echoed some of my own awkward feelings about everything. We'd been on the move since what happened in his study. What was he thinking about it?

"We should start with trying to figure out what is going on with you, Amber. Then we can look for more information on everything else." He glanced at the people around him then said, "Today is all about information."

"Oh, she'll love that." Ronnie laughed. "Information is her favorite." She elbowed me in the ribs.

"Do the creatures here speak anything other than that language you were just speaking?" I asked. "I think I'm going to need to question them about things eventually."

"Whoa, slow down a little bit." Jack put his arm around my shoulder and pulled me to his side. My heart jumped. It was so casual. Did he really not feel weird about what happened in his study? I pushed him away.

"*Oh come on,*" Lure said, exasperated.

Ronnie gave me a questioning look that said *Are you alright?*

I couldn't say anything, not with him here. For the first time, I wanted him to go away. But I also knew I needed him to make introductions and help with whatever was going on with me.

"I just need some space." I said it to Ronnie, but it was meant for Jack.

Jack's face fell, and I knew he'd understood me. My heart twinged and I wanted to take it back. I wanted to tell him that he hadn't really done anything wrong, but I couldn't. It was one too many things right now. No matter how hurt he looked or how bright and intelligent his eyes were.

"Business. Let's do what we came here to do." I took in a deep breath and focused on the gorgeous flurry of movement as creatures ran about their day. Silvaruin seemed rather idyllic, with its earthy spring smell and brightly painted buildings.

"Why don't we start with just meeting some of them first? I don't want you making enemies before we even get started; that wouldn't be wise. Come on." He stomped forward. I wasn't sure if he meant something more about making enemies or if I was just reading into things. Had I made him an enemy? If that's all it took, then he was a fool.

The creatures eyed us as we passed, and it was clear that not all of them were friendly to newcomers. I could hardly blame them. The fact that Silvaruin was even necessary was enough for me to hate humanity.

"Oh wow," I gasped. The eerie similarities to Neblig crashed into focus when we made it to the center of town. There was a fountain, similar to the one in Neblig, but rather than wrought metal, it was built of tumbling stone and five times as big. "They're the same, aren't they?"

Something dark shadowed Jack's face for a moment. Then it passed. "Different in so many ways, but with a shared history."

"What does Silvaruin mean?" I could try and translate it when I got home, but this would be faster.

"It's an old language. 'Silva' means 'of the forest' as many creatures that call Silvaruin home are. Ruin has multiple meanings, but the most important two are magic itself and 'to flee.' Though both these words use alternative spellings, the meanings are the same."

"A magical sanctuary." I nodded. "Are all these sanctuaries called Silvaruin or do they have their own names?" This town was beautiful, but I could feel the heaviness that our arrival had brought.

"No, this is a borrowed name as it is a borrowed town. Let's go to the tavern. My friends will already be there at this time of day, and they're a good place to start. Maybe they know something more." Jack led us to one of the largest buildings on the other side of the square. Most of the buildings in town were smaller homes, but this one was large and wide and I could hear merriment from inside.

We stepped inside and were greeted by enough smells and sounds to bowl me over: a hearty stew of some sort with herbs that grew among the flowers at the edge of town, the yeasty smell of bread and ale, and the various musks of twenty or thirty different persons. Jack sauntered up to the bar, leaving us at the door. They exchanged words I couldn't hear, but it gave me time to take in the tavern and its lively clientele.

They were groups of ogres, banshees, goblins, elves, fairies, and many other creatures, some I'd never heard of. I was surprised by how many of them looked like regular humans, but I knew better than to think they were. Looks could be deceiving, and I still had a feeling I was the most human creature in Silvaruin.

A group of women of all ages sat in the back corner casting stones and bones in some kind of game. I convinced myself that they weren't human bones.

What stood out the most was how relaxed everyone appeared. No one had to be worried about being found out or persecuted for who they were. It made me think of Coldwater. Perhaps Ronnie and I could turn it into a Silvaruin where no one had to hide. Even Jack looked more at ease speaking to the barkeep.

He smiled and sauntered back to us, and I swear I saw snowflakes fall from the ends of his hair. It could have just been dandruff, but I think he wasn't afraid to release a bit of his magic. It made my heart light to think of him letting go of a little bit of pain here and how he endured it in order to stay a part of the world. He didn't have to, but I imagine he did it to help the other creatures. I found myself feeling a little guilty about pushing him away.

"Our party is over there." Jack pointed at a round table with five creatures at it and four empty seats. He led us over. "Figured I'd find you here." He was in his element.

"It's nice to see you, Jack, old boy," a portly orc said. "It's truly been too long since your last visit. I know you have a job to do, but we miss you."

Jack bowed slightly to him. "Rod, the feeling is mutual to be sure, but you know I must be who I am or in the end, I am not."

Rod and the others nodded.

"These are some new friends," Jack continued. "This is Amber Dawson and Ronnie Veyl." He knew that Ronnie still went by only one of her last names. She didn't want the Murdoch name out there. They hadn't been well-liked in far too many circles for her to feel safe using it.

"As yeh know, my name is Rod." He turned to the small elven woman beside him. "Well go on then, introduce yourself. We haven't got all day, and I don't think Father Frost made this journey simply for a social call." He gave Jack a questioning look for confirmation.

"Avril," the blonde elf said. She was cute, but when she spoke, I could see her sharp teeth. Perhaps she was some variant of an elf and a vampire.

Next was a feathered woman. Her arms turned into wings and her legs were double-jointed. The black and white creature had to be a harpy. "My name is Iris." Her eyes were dark and shrewd, but I could have sworn that deep within them bubbled all the colors until they filled a void of black.

"And we're Boysen—" a male satyr said.

"—and Elder," a female satyr added.

They were obviously siblings, with their matching black and red hair and mottled fur. If I had to guess they were twins. If I weren't paying too much attention I might get them confused. Boysen was a beautiful male, and Elder was a handsome female.

"Wonderful." Jack finally took his seat and Ronnie and I followed his lead. "Now you're right, Rod, I have a larger motive in coming here, though perhaps I should visit more often if this is what you think of my visits. I'll pay more mind to coming up this way in the future."

"Oh, don't worry about it," Iris squawked. "We know you're busy, and I've heard it's quite a climb." I could hear the subtext—she didn't have to climb. I imagined flying up was significantly easier.

"What are yeh, then?" Rod asked me, looking Ronnie and me up and down, and I wondered if he was looking for scales or a tail or something.

"Excuse you, Rod," Jack jumped in before I could unfreeze my brain. "That's not a good way to phrase that."

"Who says I was trying to be nice?" He was a gruff one to be sure.

"It's alright, Jack," I laid my hand on his arm to calm him, and it seemed to work. "I'm a human, but I am trying to learn magic as much as I can."

I watched their faces, but no one gave away any amount of revulsion. I don't know what I expected, but their lack of reaction was comforting.

"And you?" Avril nodded to Ronnie.

"It's complicated." Ronnie didn't make eye contact with anyone. I reached below the table and took her hand. She squeezed mine tight. "I'm a mix of different things: human, nereid, and maybe other things? We aren't really sure. But that's something I would like to figure out at some point."

"You had ancestors that lived in the real world?" the satyr twins asked in unison.

Ronnie nodded. "Yes, though it was anything but easy for them."

"We run an organization that works with displaced and persecuted supernatural creatures," I cut in, trying my best to get the heat off Ronnie. "And we're glad to find a place like Silvaruin exists."

Jack cut back in, lowering his voice. "We do have an ulterior motive in coming here. It has to do with—"

"Neblig," Rod scoffed. "Yes, Branson told us only an hour ago. He's at Hilda's right now, but he told us all about Jetmir, and you coming to snoop around." He glared at Ronnie and me.

It was clear that Branson didn't trust us and I couldn't really blame him, but he'd stymied our investigation significantly.

"We are here to discuss the murder in Neblig, yes. We've had word of break-ins and malcontent. But we have something else to discuss too." Jack swallowed as he tried to remain calm, but the room grew a couple of degrees colder. His voice grew quieter. "Amber is having episodes, and we want to know the source."

"There have been break-ins," Elder said.

"And weird magic, too," Boysen added.

"Weird magic?" I asked. "What qualifies as weird magic?" I couldn't help but wonder if it was tied to my visions. "All of Ambrosia's plants died." Boysen scratched his right ear.

"She's a good gardener. It's either poison or magic, and who'd use poison?" Elder scratched her left ear. "It's much easier to trace."

"Do you suspect anyone?" I asked as I pulled out my notebook.

"Put that away," Iris hissed. "We may not mind sharing information with you, but there are plenty who would take offense to your snooping."

I did as she ordered and tucked my notebook away, preparing to store everything mentally. I would have to try and write it all down later and hope that it hadn't decayed too much in my mind.

"When did this start happening?" I asked, trying to get back on track.

"Late last summer," Rod grunted. "Had my shed broken into, but nothing was taken—left a huge mark on the wood though."

"Could we see it?" Jack asked. "Maybe it will tell us something about the magic that caused it."

"I guess so." Rod downed the rest of his pint of ale and sauntered over to the counter.

The others followed his lead and soon enough we'd left the tavern and headed across the square to his tall home. It was rustic and made of different kinds of wood, all jumbled together. It fit him well.

"It isn't much, but it's home," Rod said as he led us around back to a squat brick building with double wooden doors. Sure enough, there was a ring of discoloration about two feet in diameter around the handles.

"It looks like magic, that's for sure." Jack got up close to it.

"That's what I said, wasn't it?"

"Yes, yes you did." Jack didn't even seem to care about how rude Rod was.

"Would it be alright if I took a picture of this?" I asked, trying my best not to make any of them angry, but there were distinct dark patches that I wanted to zoom in on.

"Yeah, go ahead." Rod picked up a shovel and started shoving it into the ground for no apparent reason while the rest of the group looked on.

I snapped a couple of shots of the door and took as many close-ups of the odd smudges as I could. I wouldn't be able to do much more without my computer.

"Is this sort of thing highly unusual?" I asked.

"Yes," Iris answered. "We all live quite well together. It's frankly unthinkable that any of our own kind would do this, let alone commit . . . murder. Jetmir was dear to us, and whoever in Neblig did that to him is a monster." She spat the last bit out.

"I don't know," Jack said. "Aelyn and Nisse said that there were strange things happening there too."

"I don't want to make anyone upset," I said, "but I have to ask. Is there anyone who hates those in Neblig more than the rest? I know humans have treated the supernatural awfully, but has anyone been personally harmed by those in Neblig or even their ancestors."

The group looked from one to another. Someone had definitely come to mind, but for one reason or another, they were reticent to tell us. I didn't know how to make them trust me. Fortunately, after a moment's silence Avril spoke up, her sharp white teeth flashing in the sun.

"Hilda." She was quiet as though she was nervous Hilda would hear. "She's one of the oldest here, and Neblig was her home for hundreds of years. I'm honestly surprised she hasn't cast a boulder down to smash Neblig to bits by now."

"Sounds like we have someone to talk to," I said.

Ronnie's eyes were wide. "Throw a boulder down a mountain?"

Avril swallowed hard and said, "Yes, let's just say she could never fit in in Neblig."

With that, Avril led us back into the square, and I noticed Branson outside the tavern immediately. He looked smug and happy with himself. Then I heard heavy footfalls.

I turned and out of a nearby side street came a massive woman. She was no shorter than fifteen feet. It was without question Hilda the giantess. Thoughts of Old Gargy and his children ran through my mind, though she was much smaller than any of them would have been.

"Who are you?" Hilda growled. "Jack, who did you bring into our town? This is unacceptable."

Jack put out his hands and said, "Give us a moment to introduce them. These are friends. They are working to build their own sanctuary in the Americas. I brought them here to see how we do it."

"I'll tell you how we do it," she growled. "We hide away so no one will persecute and kill us, and even then they hunt us down. And you have the audacity to bring strangers into our midst and tell them of our existence."

I thought of my blog and was beyond grateful I'd chosen to obscure my whereabouts. She wouldn't take too kindly to me outing them even by accident.

She was a powder keg of a person. If she was the one who killed Jetmir, she did little to hide her true feelings. She was large enough to hoist Jetmir up onto the fountain.

I stepped forward, passing Branson, stood right in front of her and said, "What Jack has said is true. We are working to build our own sanctuary, but Jack didn't tell us about this place until absolutely necessary. I'm sure Branson has told you that Jetmir died down in Neblig." I raised my voice so those gathering around the edges of the square could hear. "He was speared on the pike of the fountain, no doubt a symbol of what you lost, and I want to help find out what happened to him if you'd let me."

"Why do you even care?" She stepped up close until I could barely see her face high above me. "We're nothing to you."

I opened my mouth to reply but before I could, Hilda disappeared from my view. It was the same wall as before, but it had a thin fracture in it that I hadn't noticed earlier. I turned around to a sea of flowers. Intense calm settled over me as I breathed in their scent. They called for me to lie down.

I turned back to the wall and could feel them tugging at my back. I pulled myself forward, one step at a time, but the wall seemed to rebuff me. I got within an inch of it. It disappeared in a flash.

The vision crumbled in front of my eyes, and the cobbled street of Silvaruin rushed up at me. Pain seared in my chest and then flared in my hand as it struck a sharp rock on the fountain. Hot, sticky blood dripped from my palm into the water.

Only it didn't dissipate as blood in water should. Instead it seemed to grow. Soon the whole fountain churned red from a single drop.

Chapter Eleven

THE FOUNTAIN FLOWED BLACK. Even Hilda seemed to shrink back a little. No—as I looked closer, I realized she was frozen. Her body was distorted through the ice. I'd worry about that in a moment. The blackened fountain felt much more pressing.

"What does it mean?" I asked to no one in particular.

Ronnie rushed up to me, but Jack was slower. Nobody answered.

"What does the black water mean?" I stared up at Jack, unblinking. Something like shock had taken over my body with everything that had transpired.

"It means you are supernatural, and you carry very potent magic." He shook his head and frowned. "I had a feeling, but I didn't realize . . ."

"Didn't realize what?" Ronnie and I asked in unison.

"The fountain only gets that dark with someone as powerful as me." He shook his head. "If someone that powerful were around, everyone in town would know. I would know. I barely even got trace amounts of magic from you. It doesn't make sense."

The crowd hadn't yet broken up, and I felt like I was in a fishbowl. My mind was spinning. How was any of this possible? Then I looked at Hilda and Branson. I was still missing parts of the story. What had happened when I disappeared from myself?

"What happened?" I asked, circling Hilda and Branson in their ice blocks. Their eyes seemed to follow me through the ice, even as it began to melt in the sun. "Why did you do this?"

"Oh, was I not supposed to protect you?" Jack asked. His words worked. I felt like an idiot. "Little good it did, though."

"Still, I didn't see what happened. " I didn't know what I did while I was gone, but Hilda's angry face frozen in the block with her hand raised told me it hadn't done me any favors. I could start to piece together how I landed on the fountain.

"You froze again. Well, not like them." Ronnie chuckled. "But you froze right in front of Hilda and she took offense to it. Before we even knew what was happening, she slapped you so hard that you flew back and hit the fountain. Jack reacted in anger and froze Hilda and Branson. He also cushioned your fall with a cold wind."

I looked at Jack, who still seemed a little hurt from me snapping at him freezing Hilda and Branson. I should have waited for the full context before going off on him.

"Thank you," I said, as I tried to extend an olive branch to him. "I was too harsh."

"Are you alright?" He brushed past my apology and the issue that caused it. "You still hit the ground pretty hard."

"I'll bruise a little but it's nothing I can't handle." I looked down at my hand and the jagged cut. "I do think my hand is going to need some attention though."

He took my hand in his and inspected the wound. Again I was surprised by the gentleness of his touch. He nodded.

"And we need to talk to someone about my visions. Whatever it is seems to be getting worse." I could see the wall clearly in my mind and feel the tug of the flowers. I steadied myself. "We have a job to do and I can't do it when I can't trust my own mind. This needs to be taken care of."

"Logical and pragmatic." Jack nodded.

Literal blushed harder than Lure. She didn't get compliments like that too often.

"Can you thaw them?" I nodded to Branson and Hilda.

"Should you?" Ronnie piped up. "Hilda did just slap Amber halfway across the square."

Jack glowered. "No, the sun can thaw them out. It's what they deserve. Give me a moment and then we can go to the apothecary. Then I have another place to go before heading home."

Jack went over to Rod and the rest of the group, leaving us to wonder what he was talking about. He seemed to be apologizing about us heading out so early. They all nodded and shared a few more words before Jack came back to us.

"They're going to handle Hilda and Branson as best they can and agree that we should get out of here before they're thawed. I'm sorry we couldn't get any more information today. We didn't make any progress." I could tell he was beating himself up.

"That's not true." I tapped my phone. "We have stories, and I have pictures. It's a start."

"Where are you taking us after the apothecary?" Ronnie blurted out. She bounced with excitement.

Jack didn't answer until he'd led us away from the crowd and the center of town. "Amber's visions seem to be coming faster and stronger than I expected, so I think it's necessary to take her to two of my friends. They might know how to help." He chewed on his lip which made me think he had something else to say, but he held back.

I reached out and took his hand with my uninjured one. If he wanted to talk, he would. For once, I didn't feel the need to press.

He squeezed my hand a little, and I took it as a thank you.

The apothecary was a tall, thin building that sat sandwiched between two other shops. Its edifice was dark, and the frosted windows gave it an ominous feel. I tried not to think the worst, but it was difficult.

Jack pushed open the door and led us inside where an owlish creature stood behind the counter with its back toward us. The building smelled of herbs and tinctures, and my head filled with the scents, making it a little hard to think.

"Oh, hello, Jack," the owlish creature said, turning around. "I should have known you were in town. Causing such commotion." The creature was jovial and nothing like his shop. Then he noticed my bloodied hand. "What have we got here?" "I tripped and fell." The lie came out of nowhere. It was hardly necessary as he'd find out what happened at the fountain soon enough, but it might get me through the conversation, which would be worth it. "Cobblestones are a lot sharper than they look."

The owl-man nodded but didn't look convinced. "Very well, come on back and I'll get you all stitched up."

He started by rubbing a poultice over the wound, and soon I couldn't feel my hand. He pulled on some glasses with long lenses and focused them over the wound.

I tried to watch his methodical movements, but I couldn't divorce the fact that it was my hand from my mind. I turned and saw Jack looking at me strangely.

"What?" I couldn't help asking.

He smiled. "You're something else, you know that?"

I blushed, which wasn't good because I needed my blood elsewhere at the moment. Lure took over, and the others were too preoccupied to stop her.

"What does that mean?" I meant to make it sweet, but it came out a bit rigid.

He laughed. "Strong, stubborn, and unpredictable."

I glanced over at Ronnie who was across the shop looking at various bottles of who-knew-what. The owl might have been listening, but he didn't seem to care or he was too focused to notice.

"Thank you," I finally said.

"For what?"

I paused. What did I want to thank him for? There were quite a few things to choose from. "For helping me. My magic is hardly the most pressing issue right now."

"I disagree. It has to do with you, so it's more important than anything."

I had to turn away as my body felt like it was on fire. This wasn't the plan.

"*He likes us. It's so clear.*" Lure giggled.

"*This is getting needlessly complicated,*" Literal huffed.

"*Oh god,*" Creativity exclaimed.

In my rush to stop looking at Jack, I accidentally turned back and saw the owl-man closing my stitches. My head went light, and for a moment, I wasn't in my body. Then everything went dark.

Cold wind caressed my face. It smelled of mint.

My eyes fluttered open, and Jack held me in his arms on a couch. We were still inside the apothecary.

"You really shouldn't have looked at your hand." He chuckled, and the motion vibrated through me. I wanted to stay in that moment, but embarrassment made me jump out of his arms. I wobbled but steadied myself.

"Where to next?" I asked, trying to move on from my fainting spell and the fact Jack must have carried me over to the couch. The owl-man seemed to have disappeared either to the back of his shop or down to the square to see what all the commotion was about.

Jack's smile faded as if he knew I was trying to ruin the moment. "We're going to see Viktor and Crow. I'm hoping they can help us."

"Who are they?" Ronnie rejoined us.

"They live off on their own in the mountains. Viktor doesn't really get along with anyone aside from Crow. He's been there for centuries and I visit occasionally, but he really doesn't appreciate it if I visit more than once or twice a decade."

"So this might not go well, then." I was becoming an imposition on him, or more of one than I already was.

"We won't know until we're there. Though I have a feeling he will find you interesting enough to get over any discomfort or frustration."

"Is Crow an actual crow, or is that just his name?" Ronnie asked as she rolled a glass bottle of herbs in her hands.

"*Her* name, and it's a bit of both. She can appear as a crow, a monster, or sometimes a woman, but that's much more rare." Jack led us outside and took us back past the edge of town and up onto the ridge.

The air grew colder until I looked back and the valley was once more just a crater of snow. I missed the spring warmth.

"This might be a strange request," Jack said, "but we need to get to Viktor and Crow's faster."

I was about to ask him what he meant, but then the ground began to move under my feet. A fissure appeared in front of me, and I stumbled back into Jack. The ground wavered for a moment, then steadily rose in a cuboid chunk.

I sat down in the snow to lower my center of gravity as the snowy crater disappeared below us. We were headed for a much larger mountain in the distance.

"You're telling me we didn't need to climb up the mountain?" I gasped as the air grew rapidly thinner.

"Just because I can do this doesn't mean I should." Jack's hair billowed in the current of wind he'd created. "We were too close to Neblig for such a clear display of my powers, and besides, it's already a risk taking you to such a high altitude so fast. The result of that would only be more severe had we flown up from Neblig."

A headache started to form as we climbed higher and higher.

"How far is it?" I asked.

"Not much farther," Jack replied as we hurtled toward a solitary mountain that stood higher than the rest, at breakneck speed. Jack was worried. I could tell.

"I'm going to be alright, you know."

Jack didn't respond as we sidled up to the side of the mountain, and the movements seemed to take a bit more of his concentration. He coaxed our floating block of ice up to the edge of a tunnel and parked it in front of the stone path carved into the side of the mountain.

I tried to stand but faltered, and he caught my arm, steadying me. He did the same for Ronnie. All three of us stepped forward onto the ledge, and the ice-lift just hung in the sky waiting for us.

"Did you have all these abilities before taking over for B, or did some of them come with the title?" I asked as we stepped into the stone tunnel.

Jack stopped for a moment and looked up and to the side as though trying to remember. "I'm not sure . . . it's been such a long time. I'm sure some of my powers came with the title, but I had winter magic before that, and I've fostered and grown my magic too. It's hard to say."

"So magical beings can increase their magic even if they are already quite powerful," Literal said.

"Does that mean magic is limitless? Is training and time all a being needs to be a god?" Creativity asked.

Lights flickered on farther down the large stone tunnel, and it grew steadily warmer as we ventured farther in away from the wind. I smelled roasting meat and heard faint music and wondered what sort of people Viktor and Crow were.

"Jack, is that you?" A smooth male voice greeted us as we neared the soft flickering light. "How long has it been?"

Jack led us through a heavy curtain into a cavernous room with a roaring fireplace and fur rugs covering the floor. In front of the hearth was a massive chair with an even larger man sitting upon it. He wore a suit made of patchwork pelts that bulged with the pressure of his muscles. He turned to face us.

Viktor made Hilda seem small.

I glanced around the room with its massive furnishings. It was a large parlor with a hallway tunnel leading farther back into the mountain. The smell of roasting meat was more concentrated in that area.

"Well?" Viktor prompted.

"Seven years, I think," Jack responded.

Viktor nodded his head, seemingly satisfied. "It isn't just a social call, is it?" His attention turned to me.

"No, it is not." Jack glanced around the room. "Is Crow here?" He seemed uncomfortable speaking to Viktor alone, which made me wonder at their history.

"She's around, perhaps checking on the meat or tending to her collections." He turned toward the hallway and barked. "Crow, we have visitors. It's Jack, and he's brought some friends and a problem!"

We all waited a moment. Then the sound of light feet broke through the silence. They shifted to wing flaps just before a three-foot-tall crow burst into the room. Her size was perfectly proportioned to Viktor, as a crow would be to a human.

She perched on the second, slightly smaller chair by the fire, and her feathers began to wiggle and expand. Within moments, she'd grown four or five times her size until a beautiful woman with a gorgeous, hooked nose and long, black locks that ended in feathers sat before us. Her dress was made of black feathers, and her eyes were the darkest midnight. She maintained much of her crow qualities even as a woman.

"Tell me your troubles." This was not the first time she'd spoken those words.

I glanced at Jack for reassurance. He nodded for me to go on.

"I'm seeing visions that I don't understand." I paused, wondering how to explain it better. "They've only started since I came to Neblig and Silvaruin. I need to get them to stop."

"Is that what you think you need?" Crow tilted her head much like a bird would. "Would you like to know what I think?" Her voice lilted like a song.

"Yes, that's why we've come," I replied as my heart began to pound.

"I think you need them to get stronger." She chittered to herself. "Yes, I think you're not the only one who's having trouble with their magic. No, no, no. Not the first. Not the last."

"What do you mean?" Ronnie cut in. I could tell she was uncomfortable with the fixation on me, but she wouldn't stop me from moving forward. "Who else is having trouble with their magic, and how do you know that's what this is about?"

"Ronnie, Crow can see things." Jack cleared his throat. "We can't sense Amber's magic, but I bet Crow can, just like Ms. Avery must have."

I could tell Ronnie wanted to say more, but she held her tongue.

"Jack." Crow's attention turned back to him. "You already know what to do. I wonder why you came here at all."

Viktor grunted. He didn't seem pleased with us being there, but his demeanor changed when he looked at Crow. He looked at her as though she were the moon herself. They were beyond happy up in the mountains by themselves. I wished I could be so too.

I looked at Jack and realized I wanted him to look at me that way. Instead he glanced at me, and all I saw was concern.

"Maybe we should go," I muttered, suddenly feeling defeated.

Jack didn't argue. He simply nodded to Viktor and Crow and backed out of the curtains.

"Is that it? Really?" Ronnie rushed after him, leaving me alone with Viktor and Crow.

"You'll figure it out," Crow said with a sweet smile. "It's not far off now." She rapidly shifted back into a bird and flew up to perch on Viktor's brawny shoulder.

I took that as my cue to leave.

"*What did that mean?*" The Originator asked.

"*Isn't it obvious?*" Literal said. "*We're going to figure out what to do about the visions.*"

"*No, she's definitely talking about Jack,*" Lure countered.

"*Or it's about solving Jetmir's murder,*" Creativity added.

"*She doesn't even know about that,*" Literal scoffed.

"*You think?*" Sadness asked. "*I wouldn't be so sure.*"

We were quiet as we stepped back onto the floating ice block, and Jack carried us as far down the mountain as he reasonably could. The wind whipped around us, but I felt no chill. Jack barely seemed to put in any effort at all.

He was more powerful than I'd considered. Perhaps I had been naive. He wasn't just Jack, he was Father Frost—a person I hardly recognized.

Chapter Twelve

"How's your hand?" Jack asked me as we crossed the threshold of his home.

"Um." I hadn't paid much attention to it with all the other things to focus on, but the moment he mentioned it, it began to throb. "It hurts, but it's manageable."

"Alright, let's get you to Amethyst, and then we have some work to do."

"Amethyst? What—"

"Work?" Ronnie asked, cutting me off. "Care to explain what you're thinking? Crow said you already knew what you have to do. Is that what this work is?"

"Look, I'll explain and show you everything in a moment, but I'd like Amethyst to take a look at her hand first."

Ronnie crossed her arms and glared at him, dissatisfied. "Sure, that's all it is. This whole thing was a waste of time, especially if Crow was right about you already knowing what to do."

"Hello, can you bring me into the conversation? This is my hand and my magic, after all." I knew they both cared about me, but I felt a little like a child with them squabbling over me like parents. "I'm standing right here."

Both of them looked at me with blank expressions, and neither apologized.

"Fine." I stuck out my tongue. If they were going to treat me like a child, I'd act like one.

"Come on, let's get you some food." Jack tried to usher me toward the kitchen, but I pushed him off and did it myself. "Amethyst will make something for you to eat, and then you'll be right as rain."

Amethyst was toiling away over the stove. She had a series of stairs and platforms to scurry about that could be disassembled if need be, but she moved with flourishes as a dance, grabbing this and that and dumping them all into a stockpot.

"You're back, good, good, dinner is almost ready. Though not quite yet." She didn't look up from what she was doing. "You will have to wait, Jack."

"I'm not looking to nick anything off you for me, but Amber here injured her hand. She needs a little something for it. Can you help us with that?" Jack opened his eyes wider in an attempt to win her over.

"Ugh, what've you gone and done now." The small sprite of a creature turned with her hands on her hips to regard us. She darted toward me and took my injured hand in her small knobby one. "Oh my. Jack, you let them do this to her?" She *tsk*ed at him. "You should have done better."

"Ameth—"

"No, I don't need an excuse." Amethyst walked away from him and grabbed a thick crusty loaf of bread. She put together a beautiful sandwich with greens and quality meat and cheese. Then she brought it back to me. "Here you are, darling, eat this up and you'll be just fine. I'm sorry about him." She glanced at him before getting back to work cooking.

"How is this going to heal my hand?" I looked up at Jack.

"Amethyst is a healer," he said. "Her food literally cures."

I didn't know how a sandwich was supposed to help, but the worst that could happen is it would fill me up before dinner. I took a bite.

Amethyst was beyond good at cooking. Images of picnics danced in my head. A memory of walking along a rocky cliff with my dad as a young girl burst forth.

He'd decided to take me on a weekend trip, just the two of us. We didn't do that all that often, but mom was away and he had taken time off work.

Now, my dad was a very forgetful man, and he didn't have any food on him aside from a strip of jerky, which I'd already devoured during our long walk. My little legs were getting tired and my tummy was rumbling, so he was just about to turn us around when we saw a building up ahead on the beach.

"Let's check it out," my dad said.

He held my hand as we picked our way down the rocks until we stepped out onto the soft sand. I smelled roasting meat, and my tummy rumbled even more.

Looking back on it, I don't know what my dad was thinking. There weren't any access roads nearby. We were in the middle of nowhere. I don't know how the little house got there, but I was a child and children have to accept a lot of things they don't understand, because much of the world is unknown to them.

I remember eating a delicious sandwich, but I can't remember the face of the person who sold it to us. It was as if their face was from an older memory, where the rest of it was brand new.

"Was that good?" Ronnie said from somewhere above me. "Look at your hand." She took my hand in hers.

"Huh?" The memory faded rapidly. The cut was barely more than a thin scar and the stitches seemed to have disappeared. "I remember hiking with my dad, but it wasn't like my visions."

"Don't worry, that's a normal . . . well, normal *magical* side effect," Jack said from a little closer. "Amethyst doesn't just cook with love."

"Does that mean she's constantly dosing us with magic?" Ronnie asked.

"I guess you could say that." Jack sounded perturbed by the thought. "Though I wouldn't. None of it is bad. Do you always know everything that is in your meal? Is someone dosing you with carrots?"

Ronnie laughed. "I can tell what a carrot looks like, but not magic."

"I wouldn't be so sure about either of those. Carrots can be blended, and you can train your eye for magic. It takes time and practice, but it's more than possible." I could feel him lean down to me. Was I on the floor? "Amber, are you doing alright?"

"You're so far away," I tried to say, but I had a feeling it came out a little bit garbled.

Jack's face came into view, and I felt his hands on my arms. "Yes, that can happen. I can help ground you." He pulled me in tight to his chest, and all I saw was white.

Gradually, the sea of white became solid and details emerged. I could see the fibers of his shirt and the light blue stitching. My brain fog dissipated, and I looked up from his chest. His eyes met mine, and I stared into their icy grey-blue depths. My stomach lurched.

"Get a room. I'm standing right here," Ronnie said, a laugh creeping into her voice.

I wriggled to get out of Jack's grip. He let me go, but I could tell he was hesitant. Fear struck me harder than any other emotion. *Am I afraid of him?*

"I'm feeling much better. I don't know what Amethyst put in that sandwich, but it did the trick." It did more than a trick. I felt like nothing bad had happened at all. I glanced at my hand and there wasn't even a scar anymore.

"Amazing, isn't she?" Jack reached down for my hand and led us down the hallway.

I thought we were going to the practice room, but he didn't stop. We passed Ronnie's room, then mine, then even the library; there were only two other rooms from there to the end of the hall, and I didn't think we were going in his room or study, though maybe he'd taken Ronnie's joke literally. The thought gave me another jolt of fear . . . or was it something else?

We stopped in front of the locked room, and Jack fished around in his pocket until he produced a key. I held my breath. He was going to unlock the door. Something about *my* blood, my supposed power, was making him unlock the door. It was almost like I was the key.

"Stand back and let me go in first." Jack pushed me back a little, blocking my view.

He opened the door just wide enough for him to slip inside. I couldn't resist. The door was opened just a crack, but I stepped forward, peering inside.

The room was dark, but I could see the illuminated door reflecting in a mirror on the far wall. It looked like a ballet studio. Why would Jack be worried about us walking into a dance studio? Was he embarrassed? The pieces didn't fit together right in my mind.

"What did Crow mean when she said we weren't the only one?" Sadness asked. I could tell she'd been sitting on the notion for a while.

"Probably exactly what she meant," Literal responded. *"Someone else isn't showing their magic but has decently potent magic. Though I wouldn't get too caught up in that because it doesn't seem like either Viktor or Crow have a good handle on time as a general concept."*

"But what if it was more recent? What if someone went up to see them about their magic?" Creativity asked. *"Maybe someone around here is dealing with the same thing we are."*

"Come on in," Jack said before I could take my thoughts further.

Ronnie and I stepped into the room as lights flickered on. It was very similar to a dance studio, but there were punching bags hanging from the ceiling and weapons lining the wall. It was a dojo.

"Care to explain this?" Ronnie asked. "I mean, are you some sort of martial artist?"

"And why did you act scared and keep this room locked up?" I added.

Jack pointed to a door on the far wall. "There are certain persons I keep in here that if let out could cause significant problems. This is a training and rehab facility. What you may not realize is that you are not the first people I have trained. In fact, Ms. Avery spent a good amount of time here." Sometimes I forgot just how old he was.

"There aren't creatures back there, are there?" My voice caught in my throat. I couldn't have this be Ms. Avery all over again. Perhaps this was where she got her ideas from. Jack kept the creatures of Silvaruin safe in order to fight other ones and use them for sick sport.

"There are some, but I promise that they are all well taken care of." He must have seen the horror on my face. "Oh, don't think that you will have to fight the creatures. No, this space is multipurpose. I have some creatures rehabilitating here, but some of them are quite wild and with all the tensions between Neblig and Silvaruin right now, I don't want them getting out. The training things are more this room and some magical artifacts. They are all training tools that aren't sentient. The creatures are here for protection and healing. Amethyst works with them extensively.

And I keep some rarer items here for safekeeping. Come, let me show it all to you."

He led us back through the door and into a solid stone tunnel. I had thought that his home was big before, but this expanded it far back into the mountain. I wondered if this was his original home.

"Is this where your house started?" I didn't need to just wonder.

"Hmm." He must have been lost in thought like me. "Oh, yes, astute observation. Yes, I used to basically live in a cave. A nice cave, but still a cave. Most of this was already here. I did do a little work on my bedroom to expand it, and certain rooms needed more work than others, but it was surprisingly good for being as is."

I could hear things moving around and see light up ahead. It was difficult not to think of the tunnels beneath Coldwater's church. I had to remind myself that it wasn't the same.

I flinched as Ronnie put a reassuring hand on my shoulder.

"Sorry, I didn't meant to—"

"No, don't worry about it." I stopped her. "Thank you." It was good to know she had an idea what I was thinking.

The air suddenly grew humid, and I smelled flowers, lots of them. Jack led us up to a window. I looked in and saw a mound of flowers, and sitting atop them was a girl. She was pale, and her left eye had a bandage over it that wrapped around her head. She was twirling a tulip in her fingers.

"What happened to her?" Just looking at her made me want to cry.

"Someone found her out." Jack's voice caught. "They were doing experiments on her and . . ."

"And they removed her eye," Ronnie said with disgust.

Jack nodded. "She's newly arrived here. I'm trying to make her comfortable, but she doesn't like the cold. I think they first picked her up in the tropics, but it's difficult to get much out of her. She doesn't really talk. I'm currently in the process of trying to get her moved to a better facility. I don't think I can give her what she needs. I'm much better with the chaotic, cold creatures."

"I wonder why." My attempt at levity fell flat.

Jack quickened his pace as if he didn't want us stopping and gawking through every window. I tried to be satisfied with what I'd already seen. It was difficult.

We stopped in front of two heavy-looking metal doors. Jack turned to me and said, "Now, what you're about to see might seem scary and awful to you, so I want to give you fair warning." My heart took a nosedive. "I'm going to try and look at your magic, not the kind you learn, but the innate kind. It may not be comfortable. You may hate me by the end of it, so now is the time to tell me if you don't want to know."

"What happens if I don't know?" He made it sound terrifying enough that even my curious self was reconsidering.

"That would depend greatly on what you are. Which of course we won't know unless I look further. But I in no way want to pressure you. I have my own bias in wanting to understand you and whatever it is that gives you next to no magical signature. It might tell us something important, but you are not an experiment, and I don't want you to feel like you are. I was hoping Crow could tell me what I need to know so we wouldn't have to do this, but . . ."

I rushed toward him before I even knew what I was doing. I buried my face in his chest and hugged him as hard as I could.

He froze for a moment, uncertain, before hugging me back.

"Thank you." I looked up at him. "You have no idea how much hearing that means to me."

"I do." I saw something in his eyes, for a moment I thought I even saw a spark of a memory alight there. Then it was gone.

"I'll do this." I tried to put on bravery I didn't feel. "I'll do what it takes, because I want to know."

Jack nodded and without another word, opened the heavy metal doors and led us into a room like nothing I'd ever seen before. Runes were carved into every surface and at its center lay a stone table carved in intricate details.

I didn't feel fear, but I did feel a massive weight threatening to crush me.

"*Is this safe?*" The Originator asked, her voice shaky.

I could feel Inner Child clinging to Literal's leg, but finding only cold pragmatism.

Jack didn't have to direct me. I knew that altar was for me.

Chapter Thirteen

I LAY ON THE cold stone altar. My mind tried to wander, but I pulled it back. We were here to figure out what was going on with me, and I couldn't let my overactive imagination ruin that. I lay still, Jack standing above me, chanting some language that must have gone along with the runes. It sounded vaguely Germanic.

"We've never really done anything magical in our life." Sadness breached my stoic defenses. It was so difficult to outpace my own mind. Some things were impossible to get away from. *"How could we possibly believe that we are magical in our very nature?"*

"Perhaps the fountain was wrong?" Creativity added. *"How do we know that the fountain doesn't just react to all blood?"*

"It could be a chemical compound in the water," Literal said. *"Though what would cause it to turn black is beyond me."*

"I think we have magic," Inner Child said.

"You also think that . . ." Literal was going to make a comeback but thought better of it. Inner Child was so often right, especially when it came to magic.

"Are you alright?" Jack leaned down and asked me, breaking from his chanting.

I didn't know how to answer. My thoughts were all over the place. It was one thing to believe in magic existing and another to be told you're some sort of magical being yourself. "I don't know," I answered honestly.

Jack nodded as though that were the answer he'd expected. "It's alright, this won't take much longer."

Had it already started? Surely, I should feel something.

He went back to chanting and the moment he stopped talking to me, my thoughts resumed. They seemed to grow stronger with every word Jack chanted.

"*Which parent?*" The Originator asked. "*Surely it isn't Mom.*"

"*It has to be Dad, then,*" Literal said.

"*Well, Mom could be a succubus,*" Creativity said with a wink, a real one, not a theoretical one.

"*What is going on?*" I asked internally. I'd never tried speaking to my thoughts before. The Originator usually translated them for me, but as I spoke in my mind, each voice distilled into a figure. I recognized them all immediately.

They were me, but their faces were slightly different from mine. Literal was a little taller and thinner, with a sharper nose and severe features. Her hair was slicked back into a tight bun that would give me a headache, and she wore a smart, well-tailored pantsuit. Creativity was quite the opposite, rounder with flowy clothes in bright shades of green and fuchsia. She had paint smeared on her cheeks and skirt, and her hair was pinned up with paintbrushes and a ruler, which I had doubts she ever used.

The Originator was the most like me, though perhaps a bit more serious and quite a bit older, middle-aged. Lure wore a fancy dress as though she were just about to go out on the town and wore way more makeup than I would ever consider—I was surprised how good it looked on my face, actually. Sadness sat in the back, flipping through notebooks, bags under her eyes. She looked as though she hadn't slept in ages. But it was my Inner Child who got me. She looked just like me in old pictures. Her large eyes and crazy shock of light auburn hair took me back to the past. For a moment I saw through her eyes, my young eyes that took in the world as I could understand it. Nothing could harm her. I wouldn't let it.

They all sat on stone chairs with runes engraved in them. It seemed that wherever I was, I hadn't forgotten the altar. I was surprisingly aware even within this inner sanctum of my being. Perhaps it was a kindred parallel with the mountain itself.

"You're so pretty." My Inner Child looked up at me.

Something within me broke a little bit. "No, you're so pretty." I picked her up and sat her on my hip. Then I turned to The Originator. "Do you know why I am here, or where here is, for that matter?"

"Your guess is as good as mine," The Originator responded. It was uncanny seeing her as she spoke.

"Perhaps I'm here so you all can help me find my magic. Is she hidden around here somewhere?" I looked for a door, or some way to find something else, but there was none. "Lure, you only showed up recently— Do you know where you came from? Do any of you know where my magic is?"

They all just stared at me. Perhaps seeing them wasn't so great after all. When I didn't see them they wouldn't stop talking, but now that I could see them, they all seemed at a loss for words.

"Perhaps we're looking at it all wrong?" The Originator said. "Perhaps she isn't an entity. Perhaps you are magic; after all, we've never seen you before."

"Wait, you can normally see each other? Does this place always exist?" I could feel my mind straining to make sense of it all.

"Not this place," Sadness stated. "Different places each time."

"Where do you go when I'm not thinking?"

They all laughed.

"You're always thinking," The Originator said over all their laughter. "Just because you don't hear us doesn't mean we've gone away. This place is new. It will be added to the places we can go. If you've seen it, we can go there."

"We try not to get separated though." Literal crossed her arms. "However, some have a tendency to wander off." She glanced over at Creativity.

"Thank you for the explanation," I began, "but I fear that doesn't get us any closer to figuring out where my magic is."

Inner Child squirmed in my arms and then placed her palm against my chest. "Right here." She smiled, and it was so difficult not to just snuggle her in closer and forget everything else. Besides, I felt like I wasn't getting anywhere.

"No, I'm Amber. Just Amber." I wanted to cry.

Inner Child began to dissolve in my grasp. I was losing them. All the while they grew fainter and farther physically, though I could still feel them in my mind. They disappeared into me until I stood in a dark room; the only thing solid was the stone beneath my feet. Perhaps I was close. Perhaps my magic was there, waiting for me in the darkness, but I couldn't see her.

"Do you know where magic is?" I called into the void. I could feel my mouth moving in a way that felt more real. "Where is magic?" I murmured it over and over.

"What is she saying?" I heard Ronnie ask.

Everything shattered. My eyes fluttered open and were blinded by the overhead light. I'd failed. I knew it. My magic was mere legend and folly. Jack didn't have to tell me, but he would anyway.

"I'm sorry, Amber." Jack held one hand and Ronnie held my other. "It didn't work. I didn't learn anything." He sounded as disappointed as I felt. "I still can't see it, but that doesn't mean it isn't there. If you're up to it, I'd like to try out your magic, and see if it will show in some other way."

"If it didn't show in here, why would it anywhere else?" I felt defeated.

"Humor me." Jack helped me to sit up on the stone slab. "Let's just get you up and standing first. There you go."

My legs were a little bit shaky, but it was really my mind, not my body, that was all mixed up. "What exactly did you do?"

"I searched your DNA, in a way." He studied my reaction.

"What does that mean? You broke me down to a DNA level?" The images in my mind were ghastly.

"In a way, yes. Though you didn't unravel physically."

Ronnie jumped in. "You didn't even move, but once you closed your eyes, you started murmuring under your breath. I've never seen anything like it."

I nodded but immediately felt nauseated. "And you found noth-ing. How could that be? Magic is somehow in my blood but not in my DNA?"

"Yes, and no. I'm not sure. I couldn't find it in your DNA, but that doesn't mean it's not there, simply that I couldn't find it." Jack looked a little helpless, something I could only imagine he didn't feel very often as the father of a whole season and range of temperatures.

"So my magic was avoiding you." *If it is there at all,* my thoughts said in unison.

"It seems so." Jack and Ronnie supported me as I stood and we walked back out into the hallway. He left Ronnie holding me upright while he shuttered the doors behind us. "We'll just do small things to see if you can do any magic at all, or if it is all . . . blocked. You've never done any magic before, right? Do you remember anything?"

"She has done magic," Ronnie said before I could. "Well, she helped me, at least."

Jack perked up. "When was this? It had to be recent, no?"

"About six months ago," I answered. "I helped her with the ritual that released the beast Ms. Avery was controlling."

Jack's eyes went wide. "That's not light magic. To undo a bond Ms. Avery made." He shook his head as he obviously contemplated what that meant. He fell into a reflective silence.

I took most of my weight off them and started walking on my own. Whatever he'd done was fading. I considered talking to them about my experience with my thoughts, but voicing it would make me seem crazy. I mean, who heard voices in their head? I'd joked about it as a writer, but no one took that seriously. I didn't either until I saw them sitting before me and held one of them in my arms. They were a metaphor come to life.

I needed time to think, away from others. Get my mind straight and figure out what was going on. I had a feeling only I could really figure out what was going on with me.

We turned off down a side tunnel until we hit a locked door. I was so thoroughly turned around by all the tunnels that I wasn't sure what direction we were facing anymore. It would be dreadfully easy to get lost.

Jack unlocked the door and led us through into the training room where he'd tried to teach us magic only a day before. Somehow we'd made it all the way back around.

My stomach growled as the smell of Amethyst's soup wafted down from the kitchen and I wondered if Jack had more than one reason for me eating the sandwich she'd made. It was as if I hadn't eaten at all. Maybe that was the price of the room, or the magic Amethyst imbued into the sandwich.

"We're going to do a really simple task." Jack pulled out some fine hemp and set it in two birds-nest kind of piles in front of Ronnie and me. They sat on the stone counter. "I want you to burn it."

"Creating fire is supposed to be simple?" I couldn't have done that easily if I had flint.

"Fire is one of the easier things for some. I of course struggle with it, but for good reasons. It's not my area, but it could be yours. Indulge me, please." He nodded to the nests and waited.

Ronnie gave me a look and shrugged. Then she set about staring at the nest in front of her. My competitiveness kicked in after a moment, and though I was tired and hungry I stared at the tinder for all I was worth, willing it to burst into flames. I imagined the tinder catching and a great blaze, but nothing happened.

I glanced over at Ronnie's pile and saw it smoldering, but it hadn't caught just yet. She wasn't finding it very easy, but that made sense. She and Harper were related. A water creature trying to pull fire from thin air was a tall order.

"Come on, Amber, stay focused," Jack said from behind me. He wanted me to succeed, but as the time stretched on, I knew it was futile.

Ronnie's hemp caught. The flame shot up for a moment, burning the whole ball in a flash, then burning out to nothing. She smiled. Then she looked over at mine, and the smile faded.

"Alright, that's enough of that." Jack snatched both pieces of hemp, the burnt and the unsullied, and disappeared to the other side of the room. I heard him opening and closing many drawers before joining us again.

He laid a block of wood in front of us this time. I looked up at him and raised my eyebrow.

"Cut it." That was all the direction he gave us.

"You can't be serious." I was so over these tasks. "These are supposed to be the simple tasks. Why don't we just call it? I can't do any of it."

A feeling of hopelessness fell over me, and I could tell Sadness was behind me, standing over me like a sickly shadow. I wanted to cry. The day had all been too much to bear.

I imagined the block split in two. I pictured it in my mind's eye, but nothing happened. Surely if my magic was so surface level to be able to do something like this without more instruction, I would have created magic before that moment.

Wood split. I looked down, but my block was still intact.

Ronnie's was split in two.

I sighed. "Can we be done now? I'm tired, and I'm done being embarrassed." It all felt like some sort of sick joke.

"I know you're tired," Jack said as he went back to the drawers. "But indulge me in one more thing, then you can rest." His focus turned to Ronnie. "I want you to try something on your own."

He pulled out a dagger and laid it on the table in front of Ronnie.

Ronnie reached for the dagger.

"No, you don't need your hands, use magic." He spun and pointed at a target on the other side of the room. "Float it across the room and lodge it in the center of the that."

"Levitation and direction?" Ronnie took a step back. "You do remember I barely trained with Ms. Avery, right?"

"Just try."

Ronnie sighed and concentrated on the dagger. It didn't budge.

Her face grew red and her muscles strained and still it didn't budge.

"Are you trying to show me that there are limits?" I muttered as Ronnie struggled. "Because it's not making me feel better if that's what you're aiming at."

"Alright, that's enough," Jack said.

Ronnie relaxed, but her face echoed my own frustration. "What was the point of that? You knew I couldn't do that."

"Precisely, but I had to be sure." Once more he went across the room to fetch supplies. "Stand here, both of you."

He took charcoal and drew a circle around us on the stone floor. Then he handed me a candle and some dried flowers. He stood back and admired his work.

"Try again."

Ronnie looked at him in disbelief but didn't argue. She strained once more.

I ducked before I even heard the knife whip through the air. It hit the target with a *thwack*.

Jack smiled and took the burned-down candle and brittle flowers from my hand. "She couldn't do that without you. She would need to grow much stronger to do what you just did."

"So I'm like a magical battery?" I could barely contain the anger burning in my chest. It threatened to overwhelm me. "Are we done here?"

"Yes, go get some rest for a little bit before dinner." He walked over to put the supplies away, oblivious to what I was feeling. "I'll come get you when it's ready."

I wanted to say more about how everyone got it wrong, but I didn't feel like talking anymore. Ronnie didn't try to stop me as I returned to my room. I curled up in a ball under the furs and tried to relax, but the tension was too real.

Magic just wasn't for me. I was an observer, an outsider, and I was okay with that. It's what made me a good writer. I should get back to what I do best.

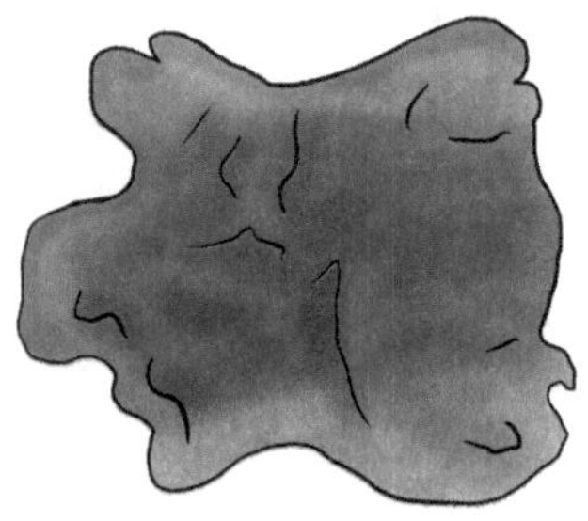

Chapter Fourteen

MY MUSCLES WERE FATIGUED. Perhaps it was just from climbing up and down the mountain, but I had a feeling it was more than that. Everything ached, and I knew it would only get worse tomorrow. I curled into a tighter ball, but even the fetal position didn't help much.

There was no sense to wallowing if it insisted on doing no good. I grasped my notebook from the side table and flipped it open. I would let Nessi's story carry me away.

Nessi spoke the words the image had shown her but she wasn't sure if they were right. There hadn't been any sound and the image disappeared as quickly as it appeared. All she had to go on was the movement of the woman's lips. The woman who looked like her and not like her parents.

Her lips moved differently from any Petrian or Flourin. It still felt strange to see herself reflected in the older woman's face.

She formed her mouth into the shapes in the fire and muttered through them. Nothing happened.

She tried again, and again, and again. Her eyelids began to flutter, but she fought off sleep.

As she lost the battle, in the last moments before dreaming, the grass at her feet began to smolder. The woman spoke the power of fire. Maybe that was the answer; if she could find power that moved the world then maybe the horizon wasn't beyond her grasp.

I leaned back and realized my chest had unknotted itself. It wasn't peace, but my body was steady. *I need to write more.*

"Amber." Jack knocked on the door.

I didn't want to answer. I wanted to send him away. No, I wanted to go away, into my mind, with my materialized thoughts. There had been something warm there, homey. I hadn't realized until I left, but it was perfect. I was just too blinded by the thought of magic to see it.

Jack knocked again. "Are you alright?"

"No," I grunted, the aches and fatigue returning as my story faded from me.

He burst through the door faster than I could think at the moment. He looked at me curled up on the bed.

"What hurts?" He sounded scared.

"It's not that serious." I lifted my head a little, but it felt heavy. "I don't feel well, but then I did climb up a mountain today, and my hand is starting to ache again."

"Can I see it? Maybe it didn't heal all the way." He held out his hand for mine.

I lifted my hand out of the warmth of the pelts. He took it in his cold ones. I flinched at the change in temperature.

"Sorry." He dropped my hand and rubbed his together for a moment, but it didn't really help. He surveyed my healed palm. "It looks normal, but I'll put some ointment on it just in case. Just try not to use that hand much." He sighed and shook his head. "Maybe I pushed too hard today."

"It's alright. I wanted to know too. It's just a disappointment that we didn't find anything new. Though to be fair, I'm not surprised. If I had magic, it would have shown itself earlier, outside of helping Ronnie last year."

"Not necessarily." I saw a memory on his face.

"What do you mean?"

He ran his fingers over his knuckles. "You're not the first person I've met with potent blood who didn't show their magic." He looked a little bit sad, but that could mean anything. I reminded myself that he'd lived longer than I could really conceive of, and misfortune and time often work side by side.

"What happened to them? Did they find their magic?" I held my breath.

"Yes, they found it." He pursed his lips and changed the subject. "Do you think you're strong enough to make it to the dining room?"

"Probably, if I have a little support." My mind was waking up a little bit, which seemed to help my body.

"Or I can bring your food in here," he suggested as I struggled to sit up.

"No, I'm not doing that to Amethyst. She's worked too hard on dinner for me not to attend." I pushed through the pain of my aching muscles.

"Amber, she'll understand." He brushed the back of his hand across my cheek.

I reached up and grabbed his hand. My heart stopped. "No. I'm going to dinner if it kills me." I gritted my teeth and stood up. I teetered a little, and he caught my arm.

He looked hurt that I'd pushed his hand away, but tried not to show it. "Alright, but you're at least taking my arm."

There was no point in resisting. He wanted to help, and I couldn't really do it on my own. I was far more worn out than even I thought. I took his arm and leaned on it a lot heavier than I wanted to. He barely even sagged under my weight.

We made it to the dining room where Ronnie was already waiting, and Jack let me settle down in the chair beside her.

"Wow, you look awful," Ronnie said.

"Thanks, just what I needed to hear."

"Sorry, I just mean that maybe you should be in bed rather than having dinner."

"Don't even try," Jack cut in. "She wouldn't let me bring her food in bed. You've got a stubborn one."

"Yeah, you're telling me." Ronnie smirked.

"Guys, I'm literally sitting right here."

Amethyst came in from the kitchen with a covered tray and set it beside the tall stockpot. "Jack, will you serve our guests?"

"Of course." Jack stood and started ladling soup into our bowls.

Amethyst cut some thick crusty bread and pattered around the table, handing us each a piece. She was so serious, but when she came up to me, she smiled.

"Oh, Jack is being too hard on you, dear. Don't be afraid to tell him no. Or even to smack him around a bit. He can take it."

"Don't worry, Amber has no problem telling me no," Jack said as he poured another bowl of soup. "She hasn't hit me yet though. Perhaps when she is a bit better we can spar a little."

How would I fight the father of winter? That would be a wildly unfair match.

"I'd pay to see that." Ronnie laughed.

"Would you stop encouraging them?" I asked. "And again, I'm right here and I'm fine, really. Let's not make this dinner all about me. What would you like to talk about, Amethyst?"

"Me?" Amethyst's eyes grew wide. Perhaps she didn't like being the center of attention. "Um, well I haven't been to Silvaruin recently. I could do with an update. How did you find it?"

Both Ronnie and I looked at Jack. He just shrugged.

"Alright, what am I missing? Now I must know."

"It was eventful," Ronnie said. "Jack froze two people, and you saw Amber's hand when we got the sandwich earlier. Didn't Jack tell you what happened?"

"No, he's not the most talkative of men, and that's saying something." She raised her eyebrows. "All he said was that you two would tell me later."

"Oh? You want our editorialization?" I asked. "Well, you saw my hand, and knowing that Jack took us to Silvaruin to try and figure out who might have killed Jetmir, you can connect the dots."

"Come on, Amber." Ronnie rolled her eyes at me. "That's not how you tell a story."

"I was just—"

"We had just come from Rod's house—the grumpy ogrish man—where we saw someone had damaged his shed, when we met up with Hilda in the square." Ronnie stood and began gesturing as she spoke. "She was angry, perhaps because Jack brought us to Silvaruin at all. Amber stepped up to talk to her, but even then I knew she wouldn't see reason."

"I was trying to see if she knew anything," I added.

"Before any of us could do anything," Ronnie continued, "Hilda smacked Amber so hard she flew across the square and landed at the edge of the fountain. She cut her hand and soon the fountain swirled with her blood."

"It turned completely black." My hand tingled with phantom pain at the thought.

Ronnie nodded. She sat back down with a satisfied look.

I was just glad she hadn't gone too far or given anything away about my visions. Maybe Jack had already told her about them, but I didn't want to share if I didn't have to.

Amethyst looked at Jack and something passed between them. She must know what the black fountain meant. "Sounds eventful indeed." She dug into her bread and soup, and we followed her lead. Maybe Jack's look told her not to pry, and if that were the case, I was grateful.

The soup was far more delicate than I had imagined. She'd blended everything up so I couldn't tell exactly what was in it, but there was definitely cheese and cooked-down wine. Whatever it was, it was delicious.

"This is wonderful," I said with a smile. "Thank you again for hosting us and for cooking. I'm afraid Ronnie and I eat out at the diner back home far too often. We've been so preoccupied with our work of late. There's always so much to do, and cooking falls to the side."

"Have you considered getting a cook?" Amethyst asked.

"Are you offering?" Truth be told, I didn't know how I'd feel about having a live-in kobold cook.

"Oh no, you're not getting Amethyst." Jack laughed.

"I can speak for myself, thank you." Amethyst gave him a curt nod. "Though he is right. You won't be getting me. I'm far too entrenched here and even Jack doesn't get me for the full year. I live in this house full-time, and I am not likely to leave it."

"That's too bad." I thought of the creatures in the locked portion of the house and her helping them with her cooking. They needed her more than anyone, it seemed. We finished up eating, and Ronnie and Jack cleared the plates. No one would hear of me helping, and truth be told, I don't think I could have. But it left Amethyst and me in the dining room alone. She slowly made her way down to my end of the table.

"Don't be too hard on yourself, dear." She put her small hand on my arm. "I know it might seem bleak right now, but your magic will come; it might just look different than you'd expect."

"What do you mean?"

She shook her head. "I don't know, dear. It's just something I feel. Most magic is past normal logic, even past where creativity can push logical thought. It's something only children can under-stand."

"Thank you for that." I wrapped my other arm around her and pulled her in for a light hug. "Hopefully I'll figure out what you mean."

"Soon enough." She nodded and then hopped down from the table and disappeared back into the kitchen. Moments later, Ronnie reemerged.

I didn't feel strong enough to limp to bed. Even without expending any magic, my energy was sapped from being a conduit for Ronnie.

"Amber, are you going back to your room?" Ronnie asked.

"Eventually." I didn't want to be a burden. I had to get my strength back soon. If I knew anything about Amethyst, it was that her food healed, and I was in a whole lot of need for some healing.

"You're not feeling up to it, are you?" Jack came back into the room and stood behind me.

I sighed, which was enough of a response for both of them. Ronnie and he shared a look. She nodded. Perhaps he mouthed something to her.

"Is it alright if I carry you back to your room?" Jack asked, coming around the side of the table so I could see him. "It was good of you to make the effort for dinner, but you need to be back in bed now."

"Fine." Hopefully, this would pass. Maybe being pampered for a little bit would help me more than hurt. However, my pride was taking a bit of a beating.

Jack lifted me from my chair and carried me bridal-style down the hallway. Ronnie stayed behind to continue helping Amethyst and I felt positively useless. But Amethyst's words rang in my head. She'd used words that were synonyms for the aspects of my thoughts: Literal, Creativity, and Inner Child. It couldn't be mere coincidence that I would see them and she would come up with the same notions in relation to my magic.

Jack carried me back to my room and laid me down on my bed. Then he stooped down to tend the fire. It was clear he wasn't planning on leaving right away.

"Jack."

He stood so quickly that he nearly hit his head on the mantel. "Yes?"

"I need to tell you something."

"What?" He sat on the side of my bed.

"When we were in that chamber earlier I saw something. I'm not sure what to make of it, but Amethyst just said something to me that makes me think it might be important." I swallowed; even Ronnie didn't know about these figments in my mind. "So. I'm a writer."

"Yes." He furrowed his brow in confusion but nodded.

"That means I observe a lot and spend a decent amount of time on my own with my thoughts." Talking about this was far more difficult than I could have imagined. "I've sectioned off my thoughts and attributed them to different fragmental personas of myself."

His lack of reaction felt strange. He was intent on listening to me with his whole attention.

"They were made up. A fun thing to amuse myself with. I've never thought much of their assertions, but when we were in that room, I saw them. I saw them in physical form, each a different aspect of myself. They were so real . . . I held my Inner Child in my arms."

His eyes grew wide, and he said, "You're crazy."

"What?" My body broke out in a cold sweat. Had I really just exposed myself so fully, only to get that response?

"I'm just kidding." He put his hand on my arm. "I'm sorry, that was unkind. But it just got so serious in here, I thought we could use some levity. That wasn't smart."

"Uh, it's okay." My fight or flight instincts would need a moment to get the message. "What do you actually think, then?"

"You saw these fragments during your vision in the room, but what did Amethyst say?" He ran his fingers through his hair, the silky strands cascading over his shoulder.

"She said my magic would be beyond where even creativity could push logic and that only a child was really capable of being in tune. Those all align specifically with a figment. Literal, Creativity, and my Inner Child. I don't know what to make of it all. Is my Inner Child the answer? Is she the magic, or is she the way to it?" My head began to pound, and I raised my hand to the side of my head as if that would help.

"Maybe we should discuss this in the morning? You've had a long day." He got up and tended to the fire.

"And what about the person who found their magic?" I didn't think I would be getting to sleep very easily. "You owe me a story." *Was it the same person that Crow had mentioned?*

Jack sighed and stretched out on the other side of the bed. "I will tell you the story, but then you go to sleep. Any other discussion will have to wait until tomorrow, deal?""Tomorrow is a day for figuring out who killed Jetmir and why my crazy little mind won't let me do magic. Tonight is for stories." I smiled. "Deal."

Jack swallowed hard. "My sister." He paused for a long time, so long I didn't think he'd start again. "She was a bit different from you because she didn't look human." He leaned back into the pillows and closed his eyes. "This was ages ago. Boreas was still my mentor. One evening he arrived back at his palace with a small bundle in his arms. It wasn't unlike him to take in those who'd been cast aside." His tone sharpened on an inhale.

I wondered if that was how Jack had ended up with Boreas too.

"He let me hold her right away and when I looked down at her, I knew I had a sister. She was an ogrish thing, and soon outgrew me, but her powers didn't come." His voice caught and he sounded as though he were holding back tears. "Boreas thought that might have been why she was abandoned, but he didn't give up hope in her. He would have taken care of her regardless of her magic."

I could feel myself dozing. "Boreas sounded like a great person."

"The best of people." Sleep was filtering into his voice too. "He helped her find her magic, but it took years, decades. And when she found it, she grew strong quickly. Her magic is still some of the most potent I've ever seen."

"Who is she?" I was nearly asleep, but the question kept me awake.

There was a long pause. I thought Jack had fallen asleep. Then he finally answered, "The witch of winter."

I tucked the name away in my mind for research later as my mind began to drift. Why would strong magic fail to come? How did Boreas free it? What walls would I need to tear down within myself to gain power? *Do I even want that kind of power?* I asked myself. Surely that sort of power would come at a cost. But I couldn't keep my curiosity at bay forever.

Chapter Fifteen

JACK'S ARMS WRAPPED AROUND me. I froze, but he wasn't cold. Between the reindeer pelts and my body heat, Jack acted as a blanket reversing my warmth back to me. I lay there. my breath shallow and my heart pounding.

How did I get here? I didn't want to move—and I wanted to run away as fast as I could.

My body was sore, but my energy had returned. That was a good start. I wouldn't be a burden anymore, and maybe I could distance myself from Jack somehow as I worked on Jetmir's case. Jack had brought me here to help, and I hadn't done anything but cause problems.

Jack shifted in his sleep, skimming his hand down my side. I shivered. How did I get into this situation? I'd been clear with my intentions of not falling for him. Then again, I'd failed in most of my intentions.

My voice was a little froggy from not using it. "Jack?"

His eyes flashed open. "Are you alright?" he asked me before he was even conscious.

"I'm fine." I squirmed as he wrapped his arms tighter around me. "I feel a lot better this morning. You were right, rest was the ticket, but I think I need some space."

He let go of me at once, and his face flushed. "I'm sorry. I . . ." He trailed off.

My heart wrenched. I didn't know what to do. I wanted to go down this path. Lure prodded me, and I could just give in to her and Jack, but I was scared.

"Should we get up and get some breakfast? We have a lot to do today." I deflected. I couldn't think straight with him in my bed.

"Do we?" He raised an eyebrow. "I think we should stay here just as we are for at least the whole morning."

He made it so difficult to ignore my feelings. "No. No, we have work to do whether you want to do it or not." I rolled away from him laughing as my nerves took over, but I rolled too far and thumped off the side of the bed.

"Amber?" Fabric rustled, and his head popped over the side of the bed, looking down at my crumpled body on the floor. "Are you alright?"

"Nothing my pride won't recover from." I pushed myself up and groaned. My muscles protested the movement, but I persisted. "We need to figure out where to begin, see who all the major players are, work on a suspect list. You did bring me here to help, right?" I tapped him on the forehead.

"Yes, I did, but maybe you should take it a little slower? Work on your book for a little bit."

I whipped around. "Did you read my journal? How dare—"

"Whoa." He put up his hands "I didn't read your journal. I just figured it might help you like it did last night. I saw you writing the other morning. It wasn't that big of a leap."

I grabbed my journal and flipped through it to a blank page. "Okay, but we still need to figure out our next move." I went over and joined him back on the bed, a dangerous move.

He scooted over to accommodate me. "I'm new to this whole investigating thing, so where do you suggest we start? It is quite exciting doing something new after so many years. It's rare."

"Glad I can help." Now that I was back in the bed, sitting cross-legged next to him, my heart started pounding.

Perhaps my mind had short-circuited before when he was holding me and now the slight distance danced with electricity between our skin. I closed the gap. I grabbed his arm and wrapped it around myself, sliding to him so we were side by side. Some of the tension dissipated, but my skin prickled where he touched me.

He looked down into my eyes. "What was that about?" He was trying his best not to break out in a grin, but it was as difficult as sitting apart from him was for me.

"How are we ever going to get anything done?" I shook my head and looked down at the blank page before me. It mocked me.

"You don't want this, right?" He nodded toward me clinging to him.

"Right." I nodded and tried to make sure my face showed the right emotion, whatever that was.

Jack lifted my chin. "If you don't want this, then why are you worried about not getting anything done? You feel nothing."

"That's not what I meant." I wish I could get my head and my heart on the same page.

"What did you mean, then?" He smirked, and everything about him drew me in.

"I don't know." It was too much all at once.

"Perhaps we should kiss?" he asked out of the blue. "It might make this all a bit easier. Then you'll know whether you want this or not."

I nodded, not trusting myself to speak. I wanted to kiss him. I wanted to give in. Maybe he was right.

He leaned in. Our lips met. His fingers ran through my curls and everywhere he touched me, I burned. His touch was cold, but that didn't stop the fire burning within.

Lure did a jig, and I tried my best not to let her take complete control of my stomach.

We pulled apart.

"I don't know how you thought that would help me think straight or figure anything out." I laughed as my emotions overlapped each other, creating a jumbled mess of excitement, fear, longing, and delight.

"I told you, we should have just stayed in bed." His morning eyes drooped and gave him the perfect puppy-dog pout.

"We are still in bed, but I said we're working today. This is called compromise." Lure groaned.

"You're intent on ruining this moment then, huh?" His smooth morning voice, intelligent eyes that whispered for me to give in, and his arms blanketed me yet kept me cool.

"How old are you?" I needed a way out, something to jog my mind and get me thinking straight.

"What does that matter?"

"Oof, that's a red flag. Jack, you're so old that you don't even really know how old you are, do you?"

"After a certain point, it doesn't matter." His voice grew soft. "Is that your objection to me? I'm too old?"

"No. No, I didn't say that. I just . . ." I didn't know how to get this all to slow down without stopping completely. If the kiss crystalized anything, it was that it wouldn't stop, no matter how hard I pushed back. "I need this to slow down. I'm not asking for it to stop. I don't think we could do that, but there is so much going on adding feelings into the mix feels like a disaster waiting to happen. I didn't have a great experience the last time I tried dating, so I need time to think and process this."

"Of course, I understand." He lifted his arm from my back, giving me space.

I felt a brief moment of panic. "No, you can leave your arm around me. I said we should slow down, not stop altogether."

He laid his arm back down and said, "Alright, so where do you want to start?"

My heart warmed. He understood and didn't hate me for my needs. "Suspects. Throw them all out, and I'll write them down until we have a complete list of all the players. Then we start ruling them out. Try not to overlook anyone no matter how much you care about or like them."

"Alright, then why don't we start with B. That's where you started, wasn't it?" He laughed, and I blushed. "Oh, no. No, that was meant as a joke. It's really alright. I would have suspected me too." He paused and then started spouting off names. "Bastien, Aelyn, Nisse, Rod, Avril, Iris, Elder and Boysen, Amethyst, Crow, and Viktor. It could be someone beyond that, but those are the people who I believe came in contact with Jetmir."

He pointed at the page in front of me. "You're not writing any of this down."

"I'm thinking, I'll jot it down in a moment." I wrote down a couple of notes and looked over them. "Now, it looks like this list heavily skews to the supernatural. Can you think of anyone in Neblig who might have it out for the supernatural? Someone who might have noticed the magical phenomenon in Neblig and decided to send a message?"

Jack rubbed his face. "I don't know. This feels like it might be related to magic. I know those in Silvaruin believe all of Neblig hates them, but this is a spiritual town. Chalandamarz celebrates certain spirits."

"If I've learned anything from the events in Coldwater, it's that you can't rule anyone out, no matter how much you might want to. However, I agree that there aren't any solid leads here."

"Even me?"

I hesitated. It would be going against my own axiom to not suspect him, but I didn't anymore. All suspicion had been assuaged. "The exception proves the rule. Ronnie was the exception in Coldwater, and you are the exception here. I trust my instincts on this."

Jack smiled, and I didn't perceive any deception in it. "So you have a list, now what?"

"Breakfast?"

He looked at me like I'd lost my mind, but of all the things that would make him think that, breakfast should have been last on the list. "I thought we had to work?"

"We also have to eat, don't we? Besides, we have to go to town and I'm not trekking down the mountain before I've had something to eat."

"You're confusing, you know that?"

I snapped my notebook shut and hopped off the bed. "Maybe. Either way, you should go to your room and get changed. I'm going to jump in the shower. Hopefully, it will help my sore limbs from our hike."

Jack laughed. "That's going to be nothing compared to later."

"Later?" I didn't even try to think what he might mean.

"You need to learn how to fight because I have a feeling you've got a tendency to get yourself into dangerous situations. We can do a little sparring, and I can teach you and Ronnie a thing or two, like how to throw a punch." I could hear the subtext, that he was worried because I didn't have magic.

"Fine." I needed a moment alone and had a feeling he would be slow to leave, so I went to the bathroom to shower. Without me in the room, it might be easier for him to get ready for the day.

"Why are we pushing him away?" Lure asked, as soon as the water started running over me.

"We have work to do," Literal responded. *"Jetmir should get just as much respect from us as Harper did, and that means figuring out who killed him."*

"And what of our magic?" Creativity asked, though she seemed a little bit subdued. *"Are we really going to just let that drop and forget about it?"*

"We couldn't forget about it if we tried," The Originator said.

I wanted to speak into my thoughts, but I was scared. I couldn't be out of commission for the whole day, and I really didn't want to pass out in the shower. That experiment would have to wait.

I tried to calm my mind and not think about anything, but that had never been easy for me. Perhaps at the very least, I could keep them at bay for a little while, push them down so they weren't so surface. I tried to remember when I first heard their voices. Perhaps it had started with just Creativity and Literal, or maybe they'd all always been there.

My head started to pound, and even the wash of water wasn't enough to calm my mind. I stepped out, dried off, and got changed. Fortunately, Jack had had the good sense to leave. I straightened my room a little and packed my bag for the trip down to Neblig. I eyed my computer and wondered if I should update my blog, but it didn't seem that important at the moment. Murder superseded everything.

I left my room and headed down to the dining room. Amethyst was banging around in the kitchen cooking. It seemed that she was happy to make breakfast for us.

Ronnie was already in the dining room, eating. I was surprised to see her up and with her nose stuck into an old book. *Had she been to Jack's library?*

"Jet lag finally wearing off?" I asked.

"No, you and Jack just stayed in your room a little later than you would normally get up. He's slowing down your anxious energy." She finally looked up with a massive grin. "I think it's a good thing."

She must have seen him leave my room. "We were working on figuring out suspects for Jetmir's murder."

"Uh-huh." She stuffed some eggs in her mouth. "I hope you put Hilda and Branson on the list."

"Oh, I didn't." I pulled out the list and added the two names. "Huh."

"What?" Ronnie looked up, intrigue in her eyes.

"It's just that I hadn't realized it before, but Jack basically only put his friends down as suspects in this case."

"Is that unrealistic? Jetmir was one of his friends. It stands to reason that there would be plenty of overlap."

"Yes, but friends and enemies are much different." I took a seat and Amethyst appeared as if my sitting had summoned her. She set a heaping plate of eggs, mini rösti, and bacon in front of me. "Thank you."

"Not really. It's very easy for a friend to become an enemy. You should know that, Amber. Look at Ms. Avery, Mr. Ward, Father Jenkins, and Harper. They were a group that did game nights, and there was enough strife among them to make anyone question their friends."

"You're right. Maybe I'm not looking at this personally enough." I set about eating, and Ronnie went back to her book. I was going to ask her what it was about, but then Jack arrived and distracted me.

"Morning," he said like we hadn't woken up in the same bed.

"Morning," Ronnie said with a smirk.

"She knows, doesn't she?" Jack asked me.

I nodded.

He sighed and sat down, but the sigh didn't match his facial expression. He was pleased he didn't have to hide it. I could tell.

We ate in silence for a little bit, and I could feel his eyes on me. Ronnie had stopped reading but held up the book as a pretense. She was waiting for us to talk.

"Who should we talk to first?" I asked. "I think this will be a different kind of investigation than the last one because you've actually been sanctioned to help investigate."

"We should go to the station and see if they've found anything new, don't you think?" Jack asked. "It's been a couple of days, I'm sure they've learned something about how Jetmir died."

"I suppose. As long as they are okay with Ronnie and me going there. I think—"

Ronnie cut me off. "Anyone want to bring me up to speed? Who is your top suspect? Also, are we forgetting that Jetmir was found impaled on the fountain?" she asked, then added, "That seems really clear to me."

Something crashed to the floor in the kitchen before either Jack or I could respond. We all shot out of our seats to make sure Amethyst was okay. She lay on the floor a bit dazed, a large pot spilled over beside her.

Jack stooped down and checked on her. After a moment of muttering quietly to her, he looked up. "It's alright. She'll be fine. She must have just slipped." Had Amethyst heard us? She was still on the suspect list. Did she fall on purpose to disrupt us somehow? Surely not. That would mean she had something serious to hide.

Chapter Sixteen

AMETHYST'S ROOM WAS JUST what I thought it would be—cluttered but in an orderly way. Amethyst was a magpie, and I had a feeling that Jack fed her addiction to baubles and bits. Every wall in the room was covered in shelves with little bottles and chests of trinkets. A dragon's hoard wasn't so well curated.

"Is she going to be alright?" Ronnie asked.

"Yes, but let's give her some space." Jack backed up but trod carefully among the trinkets.

We stood and watched her. She hadn't said much as Jack carried her to her room. Someone would need to watch because she might have gotten a concussion.

She stirred, and her eyes brightened.

"What are you all staring at?" she asked, then put her hand up to the goose egg on her head. "Ouch."

"You took a tumble," Jack said. "I think the stockpot must have hit you on the head. Do you remember what happened?"

She was slow to respond. "I'm sorry, I shouldn't have eaten them. I didn't feel well afterward, but dishes from last night needed to be put away, and breakfast needed to be made, so I thought I could push through. I don't know what's the matter with me, but it was probably the buns."

"Here," Jack grabbed the small glass on her bedside table. It was already half empty. "This'll make you feel better. What buns are you talking about?" "Thank you, dear." She took the glass in both hands and took a couple of gulps. "They were at the front door this morning, in a nice little basket, when I went to grab some potatoes. I only had one and was going to save the rest for you, but I never got to put them out. They must have really gone off."

For a moment she looked better, then she sank back into her bed, going unconscious. I looked at Ronnie. She stared tentatively at Amethyst.

"Amethyst?" Jack asked, standing over her. "Quick, Ronnie, run to the kitchen and grab the basket she described and meet me in the practice room." He reached down, scooped Amethyst up, and ran out of the room.

She had no choice but to do as he said. He made his way to the magic room with all the drawers. By the time Ronnie arrived with the basket of buns, he'd already mixed some sort of concoction and spooned it into Amethyst's mouth.

"What's going on?" I asked, though I already had an inkling.

"She's been poisoned." His voice was raw as if he were trying very hard to hold back tears. "I don't know who would do such a thing. It's truly awful."

Amethyst coughed and then retched on the table.

Jack patted her back, murmuring to her, "It's alright. Get it all out." She sat up and just stared, her breathing and pulse normal.

"Who would want to hurt Amethyst?" I asked. "Who even knows about her?" I couldn't imagine Jack telling many people about her, and she didn't go out into Neblig at all from what I knew, though she had mentioned going to Silvaruin in the past.

Jack shook his head. "I don't know, but I'm going to find out." He grabbed the buns and a container of vials. Then he started dropping a little bit of a bun into each and followed it with a bit of water.

"What are you doing?" Ronnie echoed my own question.

"Figuring out just what she was poisoned with. There are only a couple of poisons that can be used on supernatural creatures. Some will hurt humans, and others won't." He pulled the drawers open, grabbed a powder, and put it in a couple of the vials. "I can figure out what poison is in the buns by how it interacts with other herbs."

"Brilliant." It was exactly how I would do it if I had the knowledge. Perhaps that was something I could learn from Jack after fighting. He would think the fighting was more important, though, and I doubted I could sway him from that.

"Only if it works. And there are quite a few other ingredients in the buns, so we might have some false positives." He sighed.

"It'll work," Amethyst said, her eyes focusing on the world around her. "You're a smart boy, always have been. Plus there are only so many likely ingredients in a bun."

Jack smiled and blushed a little. "Thanks, Amethyst."

The first five tubes didn't react at all. The sixth, however, fizzed and gurgled. Whatever he'd put in there was the correct pairing.

"Mugwort." Jack shook his head. "We need to figure out who sent the buns. I think whoever it was knows we're getting close to figuring out who murdered Jetmir. I'm sorry you got caught up in all of this," he said to Amethyst.

"At least we all didn't eat them." She gave a weak smile. "If that happened, we'd all be in trouble."

Jack nodded. "Yes, and mugwort is not toxic to humans. Whoever did this knew what they were doing."

"And they knew I am not just human. That limits our search to Silvaruin, right?" I asked.

Jack laughed. "Not at all. Branson has probably told every supernatural creature in Neblig by now."

"You mean Aelyn and Nisse." I picked up a bun and rolled it in my hands. "She does like to bake, it seems, and I can hardly see Hilda making buns like these even if they were to kill me." I felt surprisingly calm. *Was she a magical creature that couldn't access her magic? Was it connected somehow?*

He didn't even take the time to clean everything up. He turned to Amethyst and asked, "Will you be alright here? It seems we have places to go."

"Yes, make whoever did this pay. No one should use food to harm." She glared.

He picked her up and carried her back to her room. He took the time to tuck her in and asked again if she would be alright. He was beyond worried. I could only imagine what he was feeling in that moment, torn between staying and going.

"Don't worry," Amethyst said as he joined us back in the hallway. "I'll have lunch waiting for you when you get back."

"You better not." He ducked back into the room for a moment.

The walk down to town was brisk and quiet. We were clearly on a mission. Aelyn wasn't ready for the anger that rolled off Jack.

We passed by Bastien's shop, through the center of town, then continued on toward Aelyn and Nisse's house. Jack didn't even knock.

He pushed open the door and called out, "Aelyn? Nisse? Is anyone here?"

Aelyn popped her head around the corner, her eyes wide with surprise and concern. "B, what's wrong?"

Now that we were in her home, I had no idea what we were going to do. I didn't have proof of anything and the look on Jack's face made me nervous.

"Smells like baked goods." He pushed into the kitchen. "Where are they, Aelyn?" Jack barked. I'd never seen him angry like this.

"Where are what?" The fear in her eyes was real, but I couldn't discern if it was fear of Jack or of being found out.

We followed Jack in, and there were baked goods all over the kitchen, but no buns. Though, if I were going to poison someone with baked goods I would get rid of all the evidence and write over the smell of them with more baked goods. She just seemed to have gone completely overboard.

"The buns. Buns you left on our doorstep," Jack growled. I went to step between them but Ronnie got there first. "Amethyst has been poisoned."

"Oh." Aelyn's eyes grew even wider. "Is she alright? How could that have happened?" I couldn't tell if her panic was real or not. "I did send buns to your house but I didn't poison them, I swear. Maybe someone tampered with them after Nisse dropped them off. I had him take them when he went out for a hike this morning. I often drop off baked goods. People would know that. Perhaps someone poisoned them after Nisse dropped them off."

"When did he leave this morning?" Ronnie asked.

"Around five-thirty, I think." Aelyn wiped her hands on her apron over and over again.

"So he would have likely been at the house around six." Jack paced back and forth in the kitchen, and I could feel our suspect pool dwindling. "I'll have to check with Amethyst to see what time she picked them up, but you have to know this doesn't look good for you."

"I would never do anything to harm Amethyst." Aelyn's face contorted as she fought back her emotions. "If I'd known this would happen I never would have sent the buns. It was meant as a kind gesture since I know you have guests."

"We're just collecting information right now," I said. "But please be sure to tell us if Nisse knows anything more."

"I will be sure to. As soon as he's back I'm going to ask him for a recounting of his morning." She glanced around the kitchen as though looking for a place to hide. "I would offer you something, but I imagine you are unlikely to eat at my house ever again."

"We should go," Ronnie said and crossed to the dining room.

I stepped in and grabbed Jack's hand, leading him out. We said no farewells and a part of me was sad because of it. But Aelyn was hiding something at the very least. That much was clear.

"Have you ever seen Aelyn do magic?" I asked, once we were a fair bit away from the house.

Jack paused in the middle of the street thinking. "Now that you mention it, no. I guess I always attributed it to her living in Neblig. Are you thinking she might be the one who Crow was talking about, another person who couldn't access their magic?"

I nodded. "But what would make her kill Jetmir and display him so barbarically? I mean I imagine she feels stuck, not fitting either camp." I could understand that feeling. "But it's not enough to make someone kill."

"Also, there is the matter of the random magic outbursts," Ronnie added. "Maybe we're looking at this wrong. It's not about a lack of magic but more about chaotic magic."

"Ironic," Jack said as he watched people decorate the town for the upcoming festival. "A chaotic magical being just in time for the festival that is all about casting them out."

"Here's a thought, and I'm just spitballing here," Ronnie began, "but what if the person who did this didn't know they were doing it?"

I took in what she said before responding. "I don't know. I might have thought that before this morning, but poison is intentional. The person knows and is trying to cover their tracks."

We stopped in front of Bastien's store, and Jack pulled out a piece of paper.

"I can go grab what we need." Ronnie snatched the list from him and gave me a wink. She didn't give either of us time to protest.

I wasn't going to be the one who spoke first. It had been a whirlwind of a day already and that wasn't even factoring in us waking up tangled together.

How was I supposed to know what to think?

"*Aelyn is hiding something,*" Creativity said.

"*Clearly,*" Literal added.

"*We should talk to him.*" Lure ignored Creativity. "*Ronnie gave us time alone with him and we're squandering it.*"

"Shut up, Lure," Creativity snapped. "*You need to think about something besides a guy for once. It's so singular.*"

"*What are the threads?*" The Originator asked, trying to get them back on track.

"*My magic, Jetmir's death, Amethyst's poisoning, and maybe someone else's magic that is potentially tied to magical disturbances in both Neblig and Silvaruin,*" Sadness stated dutifully.

"You didn't have a vision right there, right?" Jack interrupted my thoughts. "Is that where you go then? Your eyes go distant because your figment selves have taken over?" He must have been waiting to see if he could tell when they were present.

"You say it as though they were ghosts possessing me."

"They could be. They could be any number of things."

"No, they couldn't. They are just my thoughts. Is a mind palace a real place? No, it's a construct within the mind, as are these figures." I was seriously regretting telling him about any of it, but I'd been weak and vulnerable.

"It is actually highly debated as to whether a mind palace creates a real place."

"Now you're just making things up to annoy me."

"No, it really is debated. Amber, we need to talk about this. I think it could be tied to your . . . you know, magic." He lowered his voice. "Don't you want to know?"

I sighed. "Jack, there are more important things going on right now."

Ronnie returned with three paper grocery bags that she could barely carry. Jack took a couple and led us to a different part of town I hadn't been to before. He stopped in front of the police station and set his bags down on a low wall.

"I'll be right back." He disappeared inside.

Jack came back too quickly for much conversation. "Come on. I want to make sure Amethyst is okay." He hefted the water onto his shoulders and speed-walked through town. I could feel his anxiety at every step. There was no telling what the poisoner would do. If they broke into his house, she would be in danger. I had a feeling this would only make him more insistent on me training to fight.

Once we were out of town, he started sprinting. It was clear he cared about Amethyst a lot. It only made me like and trust him more. I felt a little guilty at ever suggesting he was like Ms. Avery.

It turned out that Amethyst was more than alright. She'd gone off to the kitchen to make lunch just like she said. Though she was moving a little slower than usual and teetering a little.

"You shouldn't be out of bed," Jack said as he unpacked the groceries and wouldn't let her help him at all.

She didn't protest too much, which attested to how she must have been feeling. The older kobold had no problem speaking her mind when she wanted to.

Ronnie and I left them to it and headed down the hall.

"What do you think of what's going on around here?" I asked.

"It's an adventure." She nudged me with her shoulder. "Isn't that what you're always looking for?"

"It's more than that. People are complicated. Magic is complicated. The whole thing is dreadfully complicated." I didn't want to complain. I wanted solutions, but complaining was easier.

"Amber, your magic will come." She stopped in front of her door and looked me in the eyes. "I know you. You will solve this case with Jetmir and restore peace to whatever is actually going on between the two towns, and you'll find your magic in the process.""You sound so sure."

"That's because I am." She opened her door and stepped through. "Now, get yourself together and jump right back into it."

I saw Jack come out of the kitchen and went up to meet him as he walked. I had everything I needed in my bag.

"Jack, we need to talk," I said, bolstered by my conversation with Ronnie.

"Yes, I know."

"Not about my magic, about the suspects and the case." I opened my notebook and showed him. "You were going to tell us what we need to know. It's time we got back to it and I have more questions than I did then."

"Alright, a deal, then. I tell you everything I know and answer all your questions. Then afterward, you let me help you with your magic a bit more." He saw my hesitation. "I promise I won't push too hard. I've learned my lesson and I can't be dealing with you injured as well as Amethyst right now."

"Deal." I held out my hand.

He shook it, and I followed him back to the magic room. He set about putting away all the test tubes, and I sat down in one of the few chairs. Ronnie joined us moments later.

"You get him to agree?" She knew me too well; even with a little nudging she knew which direction I would go.

"Yes."

Ronnie turned to Jack and asked. "And you got her to agree?"

He nodded.

"What? Are you pulling both our strings?" I didn't know when she would have gotten to him.

"Just making sure to speed up what would naturally happen." She hopped up on the counter and sat with her legs swinging. She'd found some metal bit to fiddle with during our questioning.

"Jack, can you come over here?" I asked. He'd finished cleaning up but now he was lost in thought.

He obliged but stayed standing.

"Let's start with Aelyn, why don't we? She's supernatural, right? Is Nisse as well?" I knew he'd never seen her do magic, and there was no confirmation she was magical.

"The nature of what she is means he can't be."

"You know what she is?" I gasped. "And you didn't think to tell us earlier?"

"It wasn't relevant earlier." He leaned back against the counter. "Besides, this is the first time you asked."

"Well, what is she?" Ronnie gripped the metal bauble in her hand.

"I thought it was pretty obvious, but maybe you don't know the stories." He fidgeted with his hands more than usual. I could tell he didn't like talking about his friends' secrets.

"She's an Undine."

Once again I felt stupid for not figuring it out. "That's why her apron's always wet."

Jack nodded. "Yes, she appears as a woman, but her clothes remain a little damp."

"But isn't that magic?" I asked. She didn't fit the profile. "I also can't believe it was her because she wouldn't have written those words below Jetmir's body."

"But it was a fountain," Ronnie countered. "You know, water and stuff."

I paced back and forth shaking my head. "What is the motive?" I thought about what I knew of Undine. They married human men, which made them appear human. "Maybe Nisse was cheating on her. She gave up her magic for him and then he cheated on her and now she's trying to get that power back."

"But why poison Amethyst?" Jack ran his fingers through his hair.

"I'm not sure yet." I turned to him and asked, "Did you learn anything about when Amethyst found the buns?"

Jack nodded. "Yes, it seems there was about an hour where they were outside the front door and unaccounted for before Amethyst noticed them."

"That's plenty of time for someone else to poison them too. Maybe she was being framed." It was a step backward but I'd rather take a step back than run full force in the wrong direction. "If we set Aelyn and Nisse aside for now—not completely counting them out though—who does that leave at the top of the suspect list?" I grabbed my notebook and set about recording what we knew about the top suspects.

"Bastien?" Ronnie posited. "The closest person is always high on the suspect list, right?"

"What do we know about him?" I looked up from my notes at Jack.

"He's not supernatural as far as I can tell, and I don't know if Jetmir discussed any of that part of him, but Bastien was obsessed with folklore and magic." Jack watched me write. "I just can't see him hurting Jetmir, not even if they got in a terrible fight."

I didn't want to ask, but I had to. "Do you think Bastien might have repressed magic? It stands to reason that he might if Jetmir is supernatural. They could have come to blows over it somehow."

"I don't know." Jack shook his head and sighed. I could tell this conversation was exhausting him.

I went through the rest of the suspects as quickly as I could.
Aelyn and Nisse

- Aelyn is an Undine and Nisse is human

- Friends with Bastien, Jetmir, Branson, and Jack

- Aelyn bakes and gives baked goods to Amethyst

- Nisse dropped off the poisoned buns (there is an hour

when they were not in anyone's custody)

- Resides in Neblig

Bastien
- Jetmir's brother

- Supernatural/Folklore fanatic

- Resides in Neblig

- Likely not supernatural

Rod
- Ogre

- Gruff

- Friends with Jack, Avril, Iris, Boysen, and Elder

- Resides in Silvaruin

Avril
- Elf (folkloric not Tolkien)

- Friends with Jack, Rod, Iris, Boysen, and Elder

- Resides in Silvaruin

Iris
- Harpy

- Friends with Jack, Rod, Avril, Boysen, and Elder

- Resides in Silvaruin

- Could have lifted Jetmir up onto the fountain

Boysen and Elder
- Twin satyrs/fauns depending on mythos

- Friends with Jack, Rod, Avril, and Iris

- Reside in Silvaruin

Amethyst
- Kobold (house elf)

- Lives with Jack and does housework for him and healing for the creatures being housed there

- Was poisoned with mugwort from the buns left on doorstep

Viktor and Crow
- Hermits

- Crow is actually a monster that can appear as a crow or a woman

- Either of them could have lifted Jetmir up onto the fountain

Hilda
- Giantess woman

- Slapped me across the town square and made me cut myself on the fountain revealing my supernatural blood

- Could have lifted Jetmir up onto the fountain

- Resides in Silvaruin

Branson
- Supernatural (unknown type – looks human)

- Shows up everywhere

- Bad vibes

- Goes between Silvaruin and Neblig

- Seems to be friends with Bastien, Jetmir, Aelyn, Nisse, and Hilda

Jetmir
- Supernatural (unknown type – looks human)

- Murdered with a bloody message on the fountain in Neblig (note, the fountains in both Neblig and Silvaruin seem important)

Suspect Profile
- May be having issues with their magic

- Is close enough to keep tabs on what we've learned

- Attempted to poison Jack and us, succeeded in poisoning Amethyst

- Needs to be able to get Jetmir onto the top of the fountain

"A flying creature would have an easier time of getting Jetmir to the top of the fountain," I realized as I looked at the list.

"So would someone with magic," Jack responded. "I could float someone up and spear them on top of the fountain." He cringed and I could see him reliving Jetmir's impaling. "Is there anyone we can safely rule out, or the inverse, do we have top suspects at this point?"

"I'm sorry, Amber, but I just don't know. It's difficult trying to sort through my friends to try and find a killer." His voice was strained, and I knew we were done for the day.

"It's alright. I'll ruminate on this for a while." I closed my notebook. "Perhaps I'll think of something you wouldn't have. The one thing I can say is that I think this must have been something personal and if we can figure out what each suspect wants, we might be able to determine who killed Jetmir. We just need to get to know people better without causing a stir and putting us in the killer's crosshairs."

"Well, we've already failed at that in Silvaruin," Ronnie laughed. "And with the poison."

"Does this mean it's my turn?" Jack smiled.

I sighed. "I guess."

But there was a part of me that was excited about my magic. Maybe that's why I was pushing so hard to figure out the murder. I knew I could just run away to figure out my magic and forget about it. However, one thing was certain in my mind—magic was a huge part of this mystery and I needed to figure out one to figure out the other. At the moment I straddled the line, and I had to go one direction or the other.

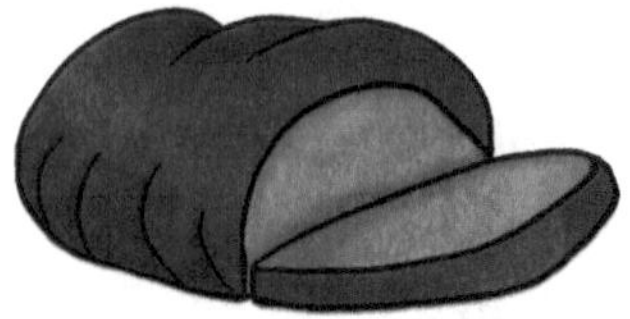

Chapter Seventeen

Only Jack knew about the people of my mind. He seemed to think they were tied to my magic too, but working that angle with Ronnie in the room would mean telling her.

Jack had me sit in a plush chair, while Ronnie sprawled out on a couch and he sat staring at me. I felt like I was in therapy. This was one of the many rooms in the tunnel complex. How he heated it all or maintained it was beyond me. The space seemed to unfold forever.

"How exactly are you going to get her magic working on her own when that big ritual didn't even work?" Ronnie asked while she sucked on a candy cane. I didn't know where she'd found it.

"I think it did work . . . a little," I said, trying to ease into the conversation.

Ronnie sat straight up. "What? You've done some magic?"

"No. No, it didn't work like that. I just saw some stuff."

"Some stuff?" She frowned. "Why are you being so tight-lipped about this?" Her eyes flashed to Jack. "Wait? Does he already know?"

"Yes, she told me this morning."

"In bed?" she asked.

"In bed," he replied.

"Oh, it's not like that. Come on." I tried to keep from blushing. "Jack, you aren't helping here."

"I know." He smirked.

"Look, I basically saw physical representations of aspects of my thoughts. Maybe it means something, maybe it doesn't, but I held my Inner Child in my arms and talked to my own Creativity."

Ronnie stared and stared at me until my skin started to itch.

"Please say something." I didn't like the silence.

"Uh, I just can't believe you told Jack about this before me. We live together. You're my best friend." She crossed her arms.

"So you don't think I'm weird?"

She gave a dry laugh. "Amber, I know you're weird, we all are. I'm just sad that you didn't tell me."

"Sorry, it never seemed that important. I've anthropomorphized my thoughts since I was a kid. I wouldn't be surprised if a lot of writers do it. It's just, with the magic and seeing them and Amethyst—"

"You mean her getting poisoned?" Ronnie asked.

"No. She told me my magic was tied to my creativity and past where logic could take me. Magic is more accessible to children. It just made me think of Literal, Creativity, and my Inner Child. I don't know how it connects, because I don't know what's blocking me."

"I hate to interrupt," Jack said, interrupting, "but maybe we should try accessing these figments? Have you had them present much lately?"

"I . . . no, not as much, honestly. They tried to show up when I was in the shower but I pushed them away and then they showed up when we were in town."

"Alright, what do you need in order for them to come out?" Jack asked.

"Calm and quiet, I guess." I sighed. "I don't know, they normally just come out. I'm thinking all the time, and I guess they're there in the background, but I don't always hear them as distinct voices."

"Okay, was there anything you did to trigger what happened yesterday?" His voice lilted. He was leaning into the monotony of therapy to the point of hypnosis.

"I talked back to them." It was such a simple thing that I'd never done before.

"Then that is where we should start. Maybe they have some ideas. They are you, after all, and you might know what is locked away inside you. They might be the vehicle for bringing it forward."

"*I could get used to him speaking us into a stupor,*" Lure said, kicking things off.

"*I didn't realize you knew such big words,*" Creativity said.

They were always there just waiting for a moment to break through. I knew my thoughts often felt magical, but that was normal for all writers; why else would we spend countless hours dedicated to jotting them all down?

"*Hello?*" I said when the other voices went silent. They were shy today as if I knew their secret. I'd trodden in hallowed halls that weren't made for me. A mind palace.

As I thought it, a vaulted room appeared in my mind. It was a palace just like the one I imagined Nessi lived in. I went straight to the library. If I knew my thoughts, that's where I'd find them.

I looked down toward my body to see if I looked like me and sure enough I was myself, but my clothes were made of thick paint strokes as if I'd been created by Van Gogh.

It took me a little while to navigate through the palace, but I'd created it so I eventually found the library. And there, within, all my thoughts waited for me, both physical and jotted down on pages. I wanted to read every book, but maybe Sadness could help me search for my magic in the pages.

"Hello," I stepped into the center of the group, and they all just eyed me.

"You've come back?" The Originator said.

"It appears that I have." I didn't know how to talk to them. They were no doubt just a manifestation of my thoughts, and this was a voyage deeper within my psyche, but I had to do something. If the reason for all this was surface level, I wouldn't be there in my mind.

"I'm trying to understand you," I said. It might be better to make this about them rather than my magic. "You've been my constant companions, a vital part of me, for as long as I can remember and yet I understand you so little."

"We've been talking a little bit since we met you in person," The Originator said. "It was a bit of a shock to realize we are just a part of your mind. We all knew it on a fundamental level, but experiencing you directly was beyond strange. So I had Sadness comb these archives." She nodded to the books around us.

"Of course you did, because you're a wiser version of me." It was exactly what I'd thought about doing.

The Originator blushed. "I don't know about that, but I do my best."

Sadness cleared her throat. "Yes, I've been looking through the books, but I read those regularly. There wasn't much new to find. However, I did go look in the vault, and that is way more interesting. I had to get special permission from two others—in this case, Creativity and The Originator—and they gladly granted it."

"She doesn't need all the backstory," Creativity said. "We don't know how long she has with us, so get to the point."

Sadness didn't look like she appreciated being rushed. "All that said, I found some memories I hadn't seen for a good long while, but they were just flashes of flowers and a stone garden wall. I heard brief snippets of whispered conversations, but I couldn't make out what was said or who was speaking. They were angry about something. We ran outside into the warm spring evening and sat in the garden among the flowers and the stars." Sadness might as well have punched me in the gut.

I flew backward as if pulled on a wire and landed in the place Sadness had described. I looked down and I was no longer adult Amber. I looked almost exactly the same age as my inner child.

The flowers and tall grass in the garden scratched my legs, but I needed to get away from the wall. It pushed me with the force of memory. I glanced back at a house I could just see over the wall.

A man stood silhouetted in the doorway. Something wasn't right. I tried to get up, but I didn't have control over my childhood body. The memory would only take the path life had taken to create it, and in the past, I must have run through the flowering field.

My breath came heavy, and the flowers seemed to grow brighter and taller. I wanted to disappear.

Even as a child, I knew it was my fault. I'd done something terrible. It was all my fault.

"*It was all my fault,*" Inner Child cried within me.

I opened my eyes, tears streaming down my face. Ronnie held my hand, but somehow remained silent. Jack's face echoed my sadness. We were silent for a moment longer as I got my bearings back in the "therapy" room.

"What did you see?" Jack finally asked, his voice soft and calming.

"I saw the figments, in a library within a castle I created, and Sadness pushed me into a memory she found." The whole sentence sounded ridiculous out loud.

"And the memory?" Jack prompted.

Ronnie rubbed my hand to reassure me.

"It was muddled. I was a kid. I ran through a field of flowers from something that I'd done. The visions are memories, ones I've buried." I began to cry. "I don't know what happened, but I know I thought it was because of me, because of something I did."

I tried to hold the sobs in, but the memory felt like an open wound, one I'd bury again if I could.

Ronnie wrapped me in a warm hug. "It's alright. You'll be alright. That's a lot to uncover, but we'll figure this all out."

I knew she was right. I knew it would pass and I could look at it objectively later, but I needed to process this in my own way, in the way I knew how.

"I need some time on my own." Writing would help me process what I'd just re-experienced. "I'm going to take the whole evening to myself."

"Understandable," Jack said. "We can do some training tomorrow, then. Hitting things might make you feel a little better."

"Maybe it will." I got up and went to leave. If I stayed in that room, I might start a panic attack, but before I got back to my room I heard a knock at the front door.

Jack was right behind me, and I let him pass me in the hall. I waited down the hallway as he opened the door.

"Branson," Jack said, his voice raising almost to a question.

"Good evening, B." His voice was soft. "I just wanted to stop by and apologize to you and your guests. Are they around?"

Ronnie bounded up behind Jack, but I was slower. Something about this made me wary. I don't know if it was Branson's friendship with Hilda or something else, but I found it difficult to like, let alone trust, him.

"Where is Hilda?" Ronnie asked. "Surely it should be her who apologizes to Amber."

Branson sighed and looked genuinely perplexed. "I tried to reason with her and get her to come with me, but she wouldn't do it. She can be quite stubborn when she wants to be. I thought maybe I could apologize on her behalf at the very least." He flipped something over in his pocket. Perhaps I'd misjudged him. He seemed nervous, and that could come across as self-importance.

"I appreciate you coming by," I said. "It would be nice to hear an apology from Hilda too, but we did leave you both frozen in ice so she didn't have much chance. If you'll excuse me, I'm quite tired." With that I turned away and went back to my room. I was glad of the apology but Branson was a bit misguided in coming alone. He wasn't the one who hurt me.

My room was calm and peaceful, which stood in perfect contrast to how my body felt. They would eventually reach equilibrium.

I unpacked my notebook, fluffed up my pillows, and settled into bed. I didn't normally write in bed, but the soft plushness was what my body needed. Maybe Ronnie had been right and I'd actually learn something from my stories.

Twilight filtered through the trees. Nessi rolled over, and something crunched beneath her. She reached down and her fingers wrapped around a small token with a human face on it. It couldn't have been there earlier, or she would have seen it when they made camp.

Her fingers brushed over it, and the world flickered around her. The forest disappeared for a moment and before her lay a field of wildflowers. The forest filtered in, blocking her view.

Someone put a hand on her shoulder. She gripped the token tight and turned around. The forest disappeared and she stood face-to-face with an older boy.

"You're a human," Nessi exclaimed. She couldn't believe she'd found them.

The boy laughed. "Yes, so are you."

"I know." Nessi bounced up and down. Then she thought of Beast and looked around for him. He was nowhere to be seen. How do I get back to him?

She tucked the token in her pocket, and the forest reappeared with Beast sleeping peacefully by the embers of their fire. She pulled out the token and went back to the boy.

"How are you doing that?" he asked.

Nessi showed him the token, holding it flat in her hand, careful not to break contact. "I found this. I was looking for you."

"For me?" The boy scrunched up his nose, puzzled.

"Not you particularly, but humans." She looked back at the tents behind him. It must have been a whole camp of humans.

The whole place was cast in twilight, so it couldn't be far from the forest.

The story had done its job and settled my emotions well enough, but I still couldn't think about the memory for very long before it threatened to pull me back into the emotional mire. My mind felt somewhere else entirely, and I floated between the created and the real world. Perhaps that was where my magic would find me.

I had no concept of time anymore.

"Amber?" Jack knocked on the door. "I have some food and a question."

"Come in." I looked up from my story and down from my thoughts, as he brought in a tray with some soup, thick crusty bread, and a glass of water.

"I had a feeling you weren't going to get proper nourishment." He looked over at the bag of animal crackers I'd been snacking on. "And it appears I was right."

"Sorry, I've just been in the zone with this story. What was your question?""Ah, yes. I want to preface this with the fact that, inviting you here, I had no intention of anything between us aside from friendship." He shook his head and I could tell he was holding back. "I've lost a lot of people over the years, it's a hazard of living so long and . . . this may be stupid to hope, but maybe if you are as powerful as the fountain would suggest, you might live longer too. I might be able to . . ." He couldn't finish the sentence.

"Is that why you're so focused on my magic and what I might be?" My heart beat a bit harder. I didn't know how to feel.

"Amber, I gave up." He pulled the desk chair over and sat a distance from me. "I gave up because it's so difficult to lose people again and again. You would think it would get easier but it never does. I say all this, because I want to get to know you. I want to go at whatever pace you want because we might just have all the time in the world." Tears filtered into his voice as he tried desperately to keep them from falling. "Will you go to dinner with me tomorrow, just the two of us?"

"I . . . Uh?" Of course I wanted to go on a date with him, but my emotions were shot and he'd just heaved his heart at my feet.

"Sorry, that was too much, wasn't it?" He backed away as if I were an injured lion about to pounce.

"A little bit, but it's okay. I appreciate your honesty and I'd love to go to dinner with you." It would be nice to talk to him alone when I didn't feel so drained. Who knows, maybe getting to know him would help somehow. I was having difficulty focusing on anything at the moment. "But I need time right now. Thank you for dinner."

He understood and left me to my musings and or maybe to my insanity. They were not mutually exclusive by any stretch of the imagination.

I jumped back into my story and tried not to get bogged down in the details. *A little prophecy, perhaps?*

"What is that on your arm?" the boy asked, pointing to a long, thin cut.

Nessi hadn't thought about it in a long time, but the moment he mentioned it, it began to itch. "It's a birthing scar." Even as she said it, she knew it wasn't right. "That's what my mom told me, but she's not my real mom. I don't know." She looked up at the boy's concerned face.

"They bled it out of you," he mumbled after a moment.

"Bled what out of me?"

"Your magic. Not all of it, but enough to make you peaceful. Enough to make you seem like them." His eyes went distant. "I've only seen it one other time on a girl, not unlike you, who came to us when I was small."

Nessi tried to hold back her tears but they came with force. "So I'll never do magic?""No. No, that's not what I meant." He reached out and took her hand. "They would have to continue bleeding you, but it doesn't look like you've been bled in quite some time. It will come back, it just needs time and proper nutrients to replenish your blood. Give it some time and when your blood has renewed, you will set the whole forest ablaze. No one will ever stop you, little one." He booped her on the nose.

Nessi thought herself too old to be booped on the nose, especially by someone who was barely older than her, but she needed him so she didn't complain.

"How do I find you for real?" she asked. "The moment I drop this token, you'll disappear."

"We'll find you."

Nessi had been literally bled of the magic; maybe that was what happened to me. Emotionally I blocked it all out. Either I'd done something terrible, or maybe my magic alone was the problem.

I lay in my bed, eyes wide open, cold soup untouched beside me. I grabbed the bread and nibbled on it; crumbs fell onto me and the bed. I did my best to wipe them off, but I wasn't paying much attention.

Sleep grasped for me. I was ready for an escape. I stood to get rid of the crumbs and looked down into the low-burning fire in the hearth.

There in the dying coals, I saw a face, my childhood face. She screamed something I couldn't hear. From her open mouth grew a poppy and a daisy. A signal, like spring, of new growth.

I plucked the flowers from the fire. They came away, corporeal in my hand.

Chapter Eighteen

THE POPPY AND DAISY sat in a cup on my nightstand when I woke. It wasn't a dream—or at least if it was, it had left real flowers behind. Either way, it amounted to the same thing. *My magic.*

I couldn't stop thinking about it as I sat on the floor of the dojo waiting to hit something.

"We should tell them, right?" Inner Child asked as I looked at Ronnie and Jack, who were discussing training regimens or something along those lines.

"Maybe we wait a little bit longer before saying anything," The Originator said. *"After all, we've only done the smallest bit of magic on our own. If it disappears again, we'll be more disappointed with them knowing than without."*

I decided to stay silent for the time being, at least until I could replicate the flowers or do something else to prove my magic to myself. It would be embarrassing if they asked me to do some magic and I failed again.

"Alright, you ready to learn how to throw a punch?" Jack asked.

"Is this really going to help?" I asked. "If I end up in a fight, I'll lose, even if I know how to throw a punch, especially since anyone who might want to do me harm probably *can* do magic."

"Come on, get up." Ronnie stepped up beside him. "Strengthening your body can only help."

"She's right." Jack stepped up to the big mirror and bent his knees to lower his center of gravity. "Let's warm up our bodies first."

We moved through different positions and soon my muscles were shaking. Neither Jack nor Ronnie broke a sweat. I very quickly found myself wishing it was evening already even if the date turned out to be awkward.

"You warmed up?" Jack asked, turning back to us.

We both nodded.

"Good. Now for the fun part." I did not like how excited he looked. "Why don't we start with the punching bags. Ronnie, I think you can practice on your own a little while I help Amber with form."

Ronnie went to the far punching bag, leaving Jack and me staring at the one in front of us.

"Go on, show me how you punch."

"I don't punch." I made no move to the bag.

"Humor me." He waved to the bag and waited.

Refusing would just make it more awkward. I looked over to Ronnie for some guidance and lowered my gravity like she did. Then I slammed my arm forward into the bag.

My wrist buckled. "Ow." I stepped back, shaking it.

"That actually wasn't terrible, though you need to engage your forearm and ball up your fist real tight." He demonstrated as he spoke, and I could see the muscle on the bottom of his forearm bulge.

I did the same thing, and nothing seemed to happen. "This is pointless."

"Amber, you won't be great at something when you've just started. That's unrealistic."

I swallowed my reply and swung again. This time my wrist didn't buckle.

"There you go." He smiled.

We spent the rest of the day working on different drills and tackling each other to the ground. Jack said it had to do with building confidence in a fight more than anything. In other words, he didn't believe that I would win in a fight either. But I did wonder if the training would help once my magic arrived in full force. I thought of it like knowing the basics of plot structure so that when an idea struck, I was ready to dive right in.

"I think that's enough for the day." Jack sighed as he stretched out his long limbs. "I'm going to check something, if you want to go get cleaned up." He headed back into the tunnels.

"I wonder how many people Jack has trained." I voiced my thoughts out loud; it was nice to be alone with Ronnie after so long with all three of us.

"Are you wondering if we're special?" Ronnie grinned.

I blushed. "No, I'm just curious."

Her face told me she didn't believe me one bit, but in very un-Ronnielike fashion, she didn't press. "I would say probably in the tens for this place, but it could be in the hundreds between here and his house in Norway. He's lived a long time, but I have a feeling that he probably does more training in the North. He's probably trained less in recent years as so many have gone into hiding."

"I wonder if he's trained Vikings."

"Come on, let's get you showered off for your date." Ronnie winked.

"How did you—"

She laughed. "It's a wonder that you doubt me knowing things. Who do you think Jack asked if you would say yes to a date?"

"I'm not discussing this." I bolted to my room and locked myself in.

I made the mistake of lying down on the floor. My whole body ached, and I was more tired than ever before.

I knew I should go and shower. Showering made everything feel better, but I couldn't pry myself up from the floor. I don't know how long I lay there.

Finally, I peeled off my sweat-stained clothing and stepped into the shower. The water felt nice, and I didn't want to leave it, but I couldn't leave Jack hanging forever.

I toweled off and dressed for dinner. There wasn't anything special about what I wore, but I had an impulse that I'd never felt before to wear some makeup. Perhaps it was seeing Lure in the flesh, but I found myself in front of Ronnie's door before I could stop myself.

She opened the door after one knock. "Oh, you look cute. How are you feeling?"

"Can I try some makeup?" My tongue felt thick and dry.

Ronnie beamed. "You're serious? Who am I kidding, I'm not questioning this." She grabbed my arm and pulled me into the room.

Powder flew and she dabbed different products onto my face at varying viscosities like I was her personal paint-by-number. She was so focused that she barely even spoke.

"There." She held up a mirror for me to admire my face.

I didn't look quite like Lure, but that was preferable. She took it too far, but Ronnie knew me well enough to realize I would only be comfortable with something subtle.

"Thank you." I got up and headed for the door.

"You're welcome, and good luck tonight," she said, her voice laden with pride.

I went searching the house to find Jack and ended up at his bedroom door. I swayed back and forth. *Maybe this is a bad idea.*

I waited in the hall, my stomach flipping over and over until I thought I might puke. It was hard enough going on a date when your date hadn't just run you through rigorous training and exercise. This was next level.

The door creaked open. Jack looked beyond handsome as he stepped out into the hall.

He was dressed fairly casually, but his normal cotton fabric shirt had been replaced by a more silky powder blue one with dark blue accent stitching. And he wore tailored black pants with leather dress shoes. Somehow our outfits matched nearly perfectly, icy blue and forest greens.

My simple green leaf-patterned dress wasn't suit-fancy. It was one of my favorites, as I only brought my favorites with me on this trip, but it wasn't my most favorite. I wasn't sure what kind of memories we were about to make, so I didn't want to sully it with anything I'd regret enough to stop wearing the dress.

"Shall we, then?" He gestured down the hallway, and I took the lead.

"I didn't think about having to walk down the mountain to get to the restaurant," I said, trying to make a little small talk so we didn't have to go the whole way in silence, though I didn't think I'd mind that too much.

"I usually don't mind it, but it might be difficult in impractical shoes. I so seldom wear these ones." I wasn't sure what to say to that so I let silence cascade over us and regretted it nearly immediately.

My heart raced faster in the silence. My thoughts were louder, and I felt too much pent-up energy that I didn't know how to release. My fingers itched for a pen and some paper, but I'd have to wait on that. If only I could release the energy as magic. Maybe I could make poppies and daisies bloom where they hadn't before. Perhaps that's all I was capable of.

We reached the restaurant, and I could feel the air zinging with energy. Something had to give: me, him, or both of us. I didn't really pay attention to anything around us. Not the restaurant name or the people within. I was barely present as Jack talked to the hostess and she led us to a secluded table in the back.

Did he ask for a secluded table, or was this his usual? I don't know that it really mattered, but it was time to talk. This was a restaurant where you didn't order anything in particular; they brought you the courses, and you ate them. A prepared menu or something like that. That meant it was fancy or touristy. Perhaps a bit of both, but Jack wouldn't bring me to a tourist place.

"What are you thinking?" he asked. There he went again, asking me what I was thinking at the most inopportune time.

"Is that the question you really want to ask? It's not done us any favors in the past." I took a sip of water and tried to steady my breathing so my voice wouldn't shake.

"Yes, I want to know what you are thinking, but I'll be more specific. What are you thinking about me right now? About the training, magic and nonmagic? About . . . ?" He couldn't finish his sentence or perhaps thought better of it. I had a feeling he was going to ask about "us." Which was a very forward thing to ask on a first date. Though we had already kissed, so it felt a little out of order.

I took a deep breath and said, "Last night I made a breakthrough. I did magic on my own." It felt good to let it all out. "For a moment this morning I thought I dreamed it but I woke up with fresh flowers on my nightstand, flowers I'd created from nothing the night before."

"Why didn't you tell me?" Jack sat back and crossed his arms, but he couldn't keep from smiling. "Can we celebrate, or is that too much?"

"I don't know, what does a celebration entail?"

"Champagne?" He smiled, and I found my heart fluttering for an entirely different reason.

"I could celebrate a little." His reaction was exactly what I needed. Somehow, he took something that seemed so small and turned it into an occasion.

Jack flagged down the waiter and ordered what I believe was their most expensive champagne. He was definitely trying to impress me, and I was perfectly happy to let him try.

"Will you tell me more?" he asked when the waiter left.

"Maybe, but I want to talk about some other things too."

"What kind of things?" He had a glint in his eyes that I was bound to disappoint.

"Murder." I couldn't help a little bit of drama. "I have a theory. It may be a shot in the dark, but all the best theories start out that way. I think something is going to happen at the festival. Which, if I'm not mistaken, starts tomorrow. Which means we're running out of time, and I'm not going to forgive myself if someone else dies or gets hurt while we're just sitting around. I feel bad enough about Amethyst, and I can only see things escalating."

"You are probably right. I trust your instincts."

The waiter came back and poured us each a glass, leaving the bottle on ice.

Jack picked up his glass and held it up to me. "To magic and mysteries."

I cracked a smile and *tink*ed my glass against his. "To magic and mysteries." It was so cheesy, I had to laugh.

We sipped our champagne, and the bubbles danced with the butterflies in my stomach. Somehow they'd captured magic in a bottle, and I had a feeling I was going to be spoiled for the rest of my life.

"So if the murder was intentional, where does that leave us?" Jack asked.

"With motive. If we can figure out our main suspect's motive for killing Jetmir, then we might be able to piece it all together."

"And our main suspects are?" Jack prompted.

"Aelyn, Nisse, Hilda, Branson, and Bastien. My gut and everything we've found is telling me that one or two of these five killed Jetmir." I took a sip of champagne. "Aelyn and Nisse are suspects because of the poisoned buns and their friendship with Jetmir. Hilda is obvious because she hates humans and, by extension, hates those who look human. Branson seems to go along with what Hilda does and is a messenger for her, so he might be implicated. Then there is Bastien, and a crime of passion between siblings."

Jack pursed his lips. "I'm unconvinced that Bastien did it. I suppose it could have been an accident, and he's remorseful, but even if that were true, it doesn't account for where they found Jetmir."

The waiter brought us our first course, a braised lamb in a red wine sauce.

"No, you're right," I said when the waiter was gone. "I don't think Bastien did it." I picked at the lamb, though I really wasn't paying that much attention. I was too focused on the murder.

"So that leaves Aelyn and Nisse and Hilda and Branson." Jack took a bite of his small portion of food. The fancy restaurant portions were comically small next to him.

"If I'm right about Aelyn's motive, then she wouldn't be working with Nisse. She's a strong contender. I think it's tied to not being able to use magic." I was certain that was a piece of it all, but something wasn't right.

We both ate and thought for a moment.

"What if Jetmir was the one who couldn't control his magic?" Jack wondered aloud. "There haven't been any disturbances since he died that I know of. Of course, that could be because the killer doesn't want to be found out, but it's also possible that Jetmir was the one who couldn't control his magic."

"That could be a motive for Aelyn and Nisse but it doesn't explain the buns. Unless they were just trying to kill us because we have the means to solve this." My heart pounded. It really felt like we were getting close. "They could have decided to put him down so they wouldn't be exposed. 'You will not drive us out,'" I quoted the message scrawled on the fountain. "It could be a direct message to Jetmir."

"We're definitely on to something." Jack's interest seemed to start to wane, and he had finished his dish. "Can I ask you about the magic you did last night?"

"It's only fair." I lay my hand on the table, and he understood and took it.

"Take your time; it was a big moment."

"I thought back to the glimpses of memories I've been having and I talked to my figments. I worked on my story, and then it all just sort of happened. I remember you came in at some point and brought me soup that I didn't eat and then, when I was going to go to sleep, I looked into the fire and saw my childhood face." The vision of my face in the fire played in my mind. "The me in the fire was screaming, and out of my open mouth, flowers grew. I plucked them from the fire and went to sleep. Then the next morning they were in a cup by my bedside. If it hadn't been for those flowers, I wouldn't have believed any of it."

"Do you ever remember dreams of doing magic?" Jack asked.

I hadn't ever even considered looking at dreams that might not have been dreams. "I don't know. I'm sure I've dreamed about doing magic. I'm a fantasy writer, so it kind of goes with the territory."

Jack smiled. "Does it? Or is it that you're a fantasy writer to process things that have actually happened?"

That one sentence flipped my whole perception upside down. I'd been writing stories for as long as I could remember. I knew that stories were often an expression of what was going on in my life or subconscious things I needed to process, but I'd never thought about my own writing giving away ideas of my magical ability. Then again, I'd only considered magic realistically six months prior.

"Now that you mention it, Ronnie suggested that my writing might be prophetic, but what you're suggesting is all about the past." I tried to square both thoughts, but all it did was bring up some interesting questions about time.

"Why can't it be both?" He squeezed my hand. "What were you writing about? You mentioned writing, so it must be important."

"I wrote about Nessi and her finding a token that took her to a human encampment. She'd seen an older human woman in the fire speaking words of power. Then she awoke early the next morning with a metal token digging into her back." I saw the scene of little Nessi awakening in the forest. "When she held the token, it took her to the encampment, where she met a boy. He noticed a scar on her arm that she'd had as long as she could remember. It was a scar where someone had bled her out of her magic. In my story, humans are magical and like gods. But there is a way for her to get it back."

"Maybe you gave yourself a way through your story," Jack said quietly, to fit the mood of the story and the restaurant's low lighting.

"Perhaps, or whatever has been blocking me for years has started to crack, just like Nessi's magic replenishing in her blood." As I thought about Nessi and my memories, deep sadness washed over me.

"What is it?" Jack moved his chair around to my side of the table so he could pull me in to him.

I tried so hard not to cry. "I think shame or guilt for something I did, or just what I was, has buried my magic deep. Maybe I won't unravel it until I look back on everything that was happening back then." I wiped a few tears from my eyes. "I'm sorry, this isn't a good date, is it?"

"This is exactly what it ought to be. I told you we would go at whatever pace you are comfortable with." He held onto me tight just like he had in his study. It had the same calming effect.

The waiter brought us a rich pale green soup and bread, and I felt more and more distant from myself. I wanted so badly to slip into the world of my mind with my friends who might hold answers.

"Can you bring us dessert boxed up and the check, please?" Jack asked the waiter. "We are in a bit of a rush." He must have realized I was done being in public.

The waiter nodded. "Of course."

"Are you alright?" Jack asked.

"I just need to—"

"—process," he finished for me. "I understand."

He ate his soup in silence and left me to mine, but he didn't leave my side of the table. I appreciated him more than ever. Though once it was quiet, my brain decided to flake on me, especially since I couldn't go into my memories until we were safely at home.

The waiter brought dessert and the bill. Jack paid it, and we left.

The chilly night air had a calming effect. I took in a couple deep breaths of mountain air, and my mind was eased a little.

"Thank you." I looked up at him.

"For what?"

"Being who you are, who I need you to be." I truly meant it. This was far more difficult than I'd ever imagined, and he was beyond perfect for me. I could feel myself giving in, and I no longer wanted to fight it.

He reached out and took my hand. I took his other hand, and we stood face-to-face in the dark beneath the stars. I could see it all before me, and maybe he was right, and we would have more time than anyone else.

I stood on my tiptoes as he leaned down to kiss me. His hand broke from mine as he lifted it to caress my cheek. Our lips met—

He pulled away from me. My eyes flashed open, and all around me were dark figures. Two or twenty. It was impossible to tell. Before my mind came down from the clouds, Jack was gone.

Chapter Nineteen

SOMEONE KIDNAPPED JACK. How had they subdued someone so powerful, and how was I going to find him?

I ran up the mountain, impractical shoes or not. I needed Ronnie more than I'd ever needed her. She'd know what to do—either her or Amethyst.

My stomach churned as images of the father of winter dying in the town center ran through my head. I had to find him before it was too late.

"*Why would they capture him?*" Literal asked. "*It just doesn't make sense.*"

"*He's gone.*" Lure paced back and forth. "*We were just getting somewhere, and now he's gone, ripped from us in the night. I want my thousand years.*"

"*Maybe the killer is trying to hobble our investigation and thinks taking Jack out of play will accomplish that,*" Creativity said. "*Or they plan to make an example of him at the festival tomorrow.*"

"If Aelyn killed Jetmir for nearly exposing the supernatural in Neblig, maybe they're worried that Jack will expose them," The Originator said. *"Or maybe Aelyn is taking Jack out so it's easier to deal with Nisse. Maybe Jetmir stood in her way."*

"It doesn't matter. We just need to find him," Inner Child pleaded.

I threw open the front door and dashed down the hall. *Where the hell is Ronnie?* I didn't even try to stop my tears.

She wasn't in her bedroom. Then I heard a noise down the hall from the sparring room. Grunts followed by thuds. I pushed open the door to see a bunch of dummies set up in the dojo at odd intervals.

Ronnie seemed to dance in her movements back and forth between them. She was in her element, and I tried to spot where she was using magic and what was pure athleticism, but it was difficult.

She noticed me come in but didn't lose her focus. "Come to join me?"

"Jack's been kidnapped," I gasped.

"Oh, shit." Ronnie took a step forward. "Are you alright?"

I thrashed my head. "This isn't about me. It's about Jack. They're going to kill him just like they killed Jetmir, and we need to find him before they do." A few tears escaped but I swiftly wiped them away.

Ronnie nodded and switched out her staff for a sword and scabbard, moving on as though I wasn't crying silently. "This won't be inconspicuous, but it's better to be armed, right?"

I grabbed a sword as well. Once they were harnessed at our hips, we ran wordlessly back to the main hallway. I made sure to lock the door behind us.

Amethyst was already waiting in the hallway. "What happened?" She hadn't been up much after her poisoning.

"Jack's been taken, and we don't know who did it. But we're gonna find out and they're going to pay." Ronnie clenched her fists.

"You stay here and stay hidden." I rested my hand on the pommel of my sword. "I think they got what they were after, but we can't be too sure."

Amethyst nodded solemnly and headed to the dojo. The creatures there were her priority.

"Can you take me to where Jack was kidnapped?" Ronnie asked once Amethyst was gone. "I want to see what you saw. Maybe we can reverse-engineer it and figure out who took him. So we need to be in the exact spot."

"What if they're watching that spot?"

Ronnie put her hand on her sword. "Then we do what we need to, but I have a feeling it won't come to that."

"You mean you will." My sword was there to deter, not to cut.

"Right."

We walked back through town in silence, which allowed my mind to go wild and my heart to beat faster and faster. I didn't have a handle on or control over anything.

"*What do you think they're doing to him?*" Sadness asked.

"*What if we could do a location spell?*" Creativity asked, ignoring Sadness. Sadness was the only one who wanted to dwell on whatever horrors Jack was facing. "*It's a shame that all we can do is produce flowers.*"

"*And we don't understand how we even do that yet,*" Literal added.

"*This is all my fault,*" Inner Child cried. I hated the pain I felt through her. Not being able to do magic wasn't her fault; it was mine.

"*At least we can strengthen Ronnie, but we haven't practiced that,*" The Originator added.

I stopped just inside town. "This is where they took him. I don't see—"

"Hush." Ronnie walked around me so we were facing each other. "Close your eyes. I want you to talk me through what happened and visualize it as you do. What were you doing when it happened?"

"We were walking from a restaurant where we'd just had a nice dinner. We left in a bit of a rush after I got emotional. We went out into the street and we kissed, then he disappeared while my eyes were closed. Whoever it was must have been waiting for us." I shook my head as the images faded from behind my eyelids.

"Don't try and figure it out. I'll think, you just experience it." Ronnie shifted and I heard the rocks scrape against each other. "Keep your eyes closed."

The evening fast-forwarded in my head until we were standing in the street and I was looking up at him. "Jack had just taken my hand. I took his other one, and we faced each other. I wasn't looking at anything other than him. We both closed our eyes, and his lips had barely touched mine when he was wrenched out of my grasp. Then we were surrounded by dark figures. It all happened so fast—""How many of them were there?" Ronnie's voice was smooth so it didn't break my sight.

"I don't—three, maybe four? I thought earlier that it had been more, maybe twenty, but it can't have been that many. It all happened so quickly."

"Did they look human?"

"They seemed to be human in stature, and none of them had extra limbs." I squinted in my mind to try and see them a little bit clearer, but it was nearly impossible to do so. I'd only seen what I'd seen. I could slow it down a little bit. It was like looking at stills from a movie. "They were . . . human, and there were four . . . no, it was one person moving very fast."

"You're sure?"

"Yes, it was one person, but it looked like more."

"Good job," Ronnie said in her normal voice. "You can open your eyes now."

"He was wrong. It wasn't Jetmir that was struggling with his magic; it was the killer." I sighed. It had been such a good theory that I wanted it to be right. "We find Jack, and we find the killer."

"Jack isn't defenseless," Ronnie tried to reassure me.

"Yeah, I know that, but this person is chaotic. That's far more dangerous."

"Do you have any idea where they might have taken him?" Ronnie did spectacularly at staying calm in moments like this.

"I think they went that way?" I pointed toward the nearest waterfall. "But I'm not sure. It was all such a blur."

"Let's get hiking, then. Movement will help, I promise." Ronnie took my hand and tugged me along after her.

Soon we were trekking along the base of the mountain. Ronnie picked up speed until we were jogging. I had to wonder if she had caught onto some sort of trail or if she needed movement like she'd said I did. Either way, it gave me hope that I desperately needed.

The waterfall grew louder and louder as we approached.

"You think he's here somewhere?" I yelled over the spray.

"Yes, I do." Ronnie barely slowed as we got right up next to the waterfall.

It splashed and sprayed us, and I wished I'd worn a rain jacket. It only took a few moments until I was soaked through.

"There." Ronnie pointed to a carve-out behind the stream of water.

It didn't look like much to me, but she went straight for it. She disappeared behind the spray and I had no choice but to follow.

It was surprisingly much quieter behind the waterfall than in front of it. The cave went farther back than I thought, and as we went on and on, the sound of the waterfall dulled.

"If this is where the person took him, Aelyn makes sense," I whispered.

"He's here."

"How do you know?" I couldn't understand her confidence.

"He's a powerful magical entity, and he must be sending off magic in pulses. I can feel it like a faint heartbeat, and it's getting louder. It was faint back in town. The mountain did a good job to dampen it, but we're on the right track."

I don't know if it was psychosomatic, but I thought I felt it too, though it was faint. I very easily could have missed it. But how was I feeling it at all? I didn't notice magic around me—not real magic, that is.

Ronnie peeked around the next corner of the cave tunnel, turned back, and put her pointer finger to her lips. I didn't know what she was seeing, and we didn't have a plan. The sword at my hip now felt extraordinarily silly.

I wanted to pull her back, but we had to save Jack. There was no other choice. We trod quietly into the room.

I clutched my hands. Jack lay unconscious on the floor.

His captor was nowhere to be seen, but we still moved as quietly as we could. I shook him gently, but he didn't stir. I checked his pulse—still there. The speed of it matched the magical pulses.

Ronnie slammed into me.

"What the—" I turned just in time to see a cloaked figure rush out at me, Ronnie on the floor. I pulled my sword. My hand was shaking, but it slowed the person down. "Get back," I yelled, fear fueling my rage. "I ought to run this right through you."

The figure backed away, and as they did, I saw a silver pendant swinging from their neck. It caught in the light for a brief moment before disappearing back into the folds of their robes.

I must have paused for too long. The person knew I wouldn't do it. They lunged toward Jack. All I could think about was him.

"*Protect Jack*," Lure screamed. The others echoed her cry.

I dove between the cloaked figure and Jack, shielding him with my body. Stone cracked. *This is it. We'll be trapped in this cave forever.*

I closed my eyes and clung to Jack's cold form. Muffled footsteps moved away from me, toward the waterfall. I could sense fear in their patter. Then all was silent.

"Oh wow," Ronnie gasped.

I pulled myself up from Jack, expecting the worst. I couldn't see anything. The cave must have been lit artificially by the captor. Ronnie already had her phone out, and her flashlight flickered on. It revealed a layer of woven wood, vines, and flowers.

A dome of nature surrounded us. The wood seemed to have broken through the stone floor. That's what I'd heard, not the cave falling in around us.

"Did I do that?" I muttered, scarcely believing it.

Ronnie smiled. "Well I definitely didn't, and I don't think Jack can do more than pulse right now."

I plucked a daisy and tucked it into my pocket. Maybe my magic revealed itself at times of great need, or maybe the wall had started to break down. Either way, I was more confident than any combat training could have made me.

"Let's get him home." All that mattered for a moment was that he was safe. Once he was home and safe, we could figure out what really happened. Perhaps the murderer had made a mistake and left clues. They never should have captured Jack.

Chapter Twenty

A LAKE OF TEA was not enough to calm my nerves or warm me up. Jack told me everything would be alright, but I was more shaken up about his kidnapping than I'd thought I was. He shouldn't be the one consoling me, but he insisted he was fine. Whatever his captor had given him wore off shortly after we'd arrived home, and Amethyst's food did the rest.

I sat in the library's little sitting room and waited for him to return. I hadn't wanted him to leave my sight again. I took lots of deep breaths, and Ronnie held my hand, reassuring me that he'd be right back and nothing would harm him inside his house. I wasn't so sure.

Jack finally returned with a tray of tea and a serious expression. "I'm sorry I made you worry." He apologized to me—actually apologized to me for something that was so far from being his fault.

"It's not your fault. That belongs to whoever killed Jetmir and decided to kidnap you." I took my tea in shaking hands. I was livid. "They're going to pay."

"Amber, I'm safe now," Jack said. "Besides, they will get what's coming to them. I'll make sure of it. "

"Do you remember what happened?" I tried not to let my mind go further down that dark path.

"I remember us leaving the restaurant, getting pulled away from you, and then, nothing. I feel like someone took a hammer to my head and I feel weak, magically speaking. I'll admit I'm a bit shaken." He stared into his teacup and then looked up at me. "I should have been able to get away, but whoever it was knew how to neutralize me." He clenched his empty hand.

"Maybe that's what they were going for," Ronnie suggested. "You have to admit you're quite a threat, and anyone trying to misuse magic would want you out of the way, right?"

"That seems like a huge risk for not much gain." I couldn't quite believe it. "Can you think of anything else that might be the reason?"

"No, not really. Maybe there was some sort of clue; walk me through what happened in the cave." He took a sip of his tea even though mine was still too hot to drink. I had a feeling his hands had an overly cooling effect, so he had to drink it quicker lest it go cold. He seemed more in control of himself than I felt. Then again, he'd been out for most of it and didn't have to feel what I'd felt.

"Ronnie could feel a pulse coming from you that led us to one of the waterfalls," I began. "Deep in the cave behind it we found you unconscious on the floor."

"You were alone, or so we thought," Ronnie added. "Out of a deeper recess of the cave came a cloaked figure. They attacked us and . . ." Ronnie pointed at me dramatically.

"I used my magic, not just a couple flowers in the fire either. I created a dome of woody foliage that protected us like a cage." My heart swelled with pride.

"That's amazing." He leaned forward and clasped my hands.

I glanced at Ronnie, and he pulled back a little.

"No need to be shy." She laughed. Then she pulled out her phone, redirecting attention, and showed it to Jack. "I took a picture of what she made."

She'd snapped some photos of the nature dome on her phone before we hauled Jack's barely conscious self up the mountain.

"Fascinating." Jack turned his attention back to me. "Did you have a memory with it? What happened?"

"Don't get too excited." I looked down at our hands. "I haven't been able to do any magic since. It must have just come out of desperation."

"Then we need to make you desperate." Jack seemed completely serious, which scared me.

"Or we should move on and figure out who kidnapped you." I didn't want to be put in dangerous situations, or situations where someone I cared about was in danger. "And we need to know why."

"Aelyn is an Undine, right?" Ronnie asked.

"Yes?" Jack said.

"They're tied to waterfalls. Maybe it was her, and she sought to bind you behind the waterfall to sap your strength," Ronnie suggested. "Then we interrupted her before she could finish."

"For what purpose?" Jack twisted his hair. "You really think Aelyn is having trouble with her magic?"

"Maybe the magic didn't work anyway." I could feel my brain overheating. "I think something is going to happen tomorrow. If it hadn't been the plan before, I think we've just expedited their plan."

"The festival's tomorrow," Ronnie added. "We're running out of time. I agree if something else is going to happen, it's bound to happen then."

"What if Jack wasn't meant as just a hostage to keep from spoiling their plan? What if he was a scapegoat? Maybe the killer planned to frame him."

Ronnie's eyes grew wide. "That's why they tried to capture him before the festival. When else would they kill a vengeful winter spirit?" She gave Jack a pointed look.

"It is Aelyn, isn't it?" Jack's eyes were sad. "She tried to poison me and maybe would have made it look like I was remorseful for killing Jetmir and killed myself because of it. When that didn't work she decided to frame me at the festival. What does that mean next?"

"Nothing good." I swallowed. "We need to be at that festival, waiting before anyone else can arrive. She's escalated twice now and is behaving more and more erratically."

"That means we all need to sleep." Jack suddenly looked tired, and I wondered if he'd done something to stay more alert and awake. "It's far too late, and we're all far too drained. We need to be at our best for tomorrow."

The library books seemed to whisper to me now that my thoughts had started to coagulate and form something semisolid. Were they trying to tell me something? "Are these books magical? Outside of books' usual magical nature, that is."

He paused and raised an eyebrow before saying, "Yes, some of them have been imbued with magic, though they vary in potency and power. Can you tell which ones are which?"

I stood and crossed the room to a particular tome that seemed to hum. It was strange that I hadn't noticed it the first two times I'd been in the library. Maybe it meant my magic was starting to show itself, just like the way I could sense the rhythm of Jack's magic tonight. My walls were crumbling, and this was magic that I didn't need to be in danger for.

I pulled the book off the shelf. "This one is humming."

Jack smiled. "Yes, that is an old grimoire. Why don't you open it up and see if you can read it? Though don't read it out loud."

I did as he suggested and recognized the same runic symbols from the room where he'd tested my magic, and from the box that held the letters I'd sent him. I couldn't read them then, so why did I try now? I stared at the pages, willing them to show me something, to prove to myself that I could access magic beyond whispering vines and flowers.

I stared so hard that the runes swam before my eyes.

"It's alright if you can't read it. Most can't," Jack said after a few minutes of my staring.

As if in defiance, the runes took the shape of letters in my mind though they hadn't changed on the page. The language felt old and full of power. The passage I was reading was about messages, specifically sending messages over vast distances by having them hitch a ride on waves of light.

"All you must do is speak your message to the light then extinguish it. When your intended ignites a new light, your message will release and join them as it ought." I read the paragraph, not the spell, and I translated it to English, though the older language was there too. I could have spoken it just as easily.

Jack looked as though he was going to cry, but I couldn't understand why. I knew I'd done something strange and beautiful, but it was clear Jack was the only one who understood the full weight of my words. I wished to dwell on it a little bit longer, but there wasn't time.

"My magic is leaking through. I couldn't feel the book's magic before today." My voice was quiet because I could scarcely believe my own accomplishments. "Protecting you must have taken a huge hole out of the blockage."

"Perhaps." His expression didn't reveal much. "I think there is still a lot that we don't know."

I set the grimoire down on the table beside me and took a seat. It was power, and I wanted to keep that close. It could keep me safe, and who wouldn't want that? For a brief moment I thought about Aelyn and felt a little sorry for her. If she really couldn't do magic, that meant she was like me, but her other possible motive couldn't let me pity her. Murder was not the answer.

Ronnie yawned, and Jack jumped into motion.

He took the tea tray back down the hall and left us alone. Ronnie watched me as I tucked the old grimoire into my bag. It may come in handy. Besides, I wasn't stealing it, just checking it out from the library.

Chapter Twenty-One

THE GRIMOIRE SAT HEAVY in my backpack along with my other supplies, and I wished for nothing more than to get it out and read more of it. The spells called to me all the more now, almost as if they knew I could read them. I didn't know what had changed, but maybe I'd done just enough to break a crack in the barrier within me.

I rushed down the hallway and found Jack and Ronnie already eating. Amethyst must have been up quite early, as a bountiful feast was laid out and the sun hadn't even risen yet. There were sugary buns, fruity jams with floral notes, sausage links, and plenty of rösti.

"How are you doing this morning?" I asked Jack as I set down my bag and took a seat.

"Quite well, I think." He took a bite of a bun and I could tell that both he and Ronnie were eating quickly. We were in a rush. "I still feel a bit drained. Whatever Aelyn did to me hasn't quite worn off."

"You don't think . . ." A horrifying thought hit me.

"What?" Jack furrowed his eyebrows.

"What if Aelyn . . . I don't know, did something to you that will make you go feral at the festival?" I had images in my head of a sleeper agent suddenly coming alive.

"I think whatever she did wasn't complete," Ronnie tried to reassure me.

We all dug into the bountiful feast, which only gave my mind time to run wild.

"*She could still be planning to use Jack as a scapegoat for Jetmir,*" Lure said, concern dripping in her voice. "*We need to protect him. He shouldn't go to Neblig.*"

"*Let's be realistic,*" Literal countered. "*We can't stop Jack from going. Besides, we might need him to contain Aelyn. Our magic is as unreliable as hers, maybe more so.*"

"*What is her plan though?*" Creativity asked. "*I can't figure it out.*"

"*Maybe she'll confess to the murder,*" Inner Child guessed.

"*I highly doubt that.*" Literal was in a mood, but then, when wasn't she? "*She's done everything she can to not get caught, even going so far as poison and kidnapping. No, this is going to be heinous, not heroic.*"

"What does the festival look like?" I asked. I needed to guide my thoughts in a more constructive direction. "I need an idea of what we might be stepping into."

"It starts with the first bell, which should toll any moment now. The boys of the village will ring bells and process through town wearing traditional Alpine and Romansch clothing. This is to ward off the vengeful winter spirits, wake the sleeping spring spirits, and proclaim spring has come. Neblig will wake to the sound and flood the streets and the festival begins. They often have vendors, and the local shops will have food and drink out on their porches. Then in the evening, there is a big party with singing and dancing. The singing goes from sunset to sunrise.""When do you think Aelyn would strike?" I asked.

"During the procession as they get into the center of town." Jack waved for me to get up. "She chose to display Jetmir's body in the center of town for a reason. She'll want to make a scene at the peak when everyone is in the square. We need to be there waiting. It's the only chance we have at stopping her."

Jack stepped out for a moment to get his bag. I stuffed a bun in my mouth, knowing I'd need the extra energy and hoping Amethyst had added some extra health into it for us. Then Ronnie and I headed outside, just as dawn was breaking over the mountains.

"How do you feel about all of this?" Ronnie asked.

"I think this is going to be worse than confronting Ms. Avery. It's going to be a lot more public."

Ronnie nodded, and I went over to the rock on the ridge and looked down into Neblig. The first bell tolled. A moment later, I could see boys processing through town in blue and red. The faint sound of a chorus of ringing bells rose to meet me. It had started.

Jack joined us, and we headed down the mountain to town. People lined every street, and the air was perfumed with the smell of pastries, chocolate and dried flowers from the previous year.

I wanted to enjoy the festival, but that wasn't going to be possible. We had work to do. Jack led the way, his tall form making it easier to cut through the crowds lining the streets. It was clear that everyone and their mother was out for the festival, and it was fun to think about other villages in the Alps celebrating at the same time. This was supposed to be a joyous festival, but all I felt was dread.

Bells rang all around us as we made it to the center of town. The chorus of ringing made it feel as though Neblig was under attack.

I scanned the crowd looking for Aelyn or anyone I knew, but there was no one I recognized until we reached Bastien's store. He sat out on his porch, Jetmir's chair empty beside him. He looked forlorn, and I knew that feeling. It was the feeling of loss during a holiday. You got so used to spending time with someone that each special moment you shared comes into sharp focus on a holiday.

Where did that thought come from? I knew that pain, but why?

I shook my head and focused back on Bastien. I could easily imagine the two of them sitting and watching the festivities together. Without Jetmir, Bastien looked lost. I don't know how anyone could suspect him at all. It was natural to suspect the closest person to the victim, but Bastien was clearly grieving.

"*Why would Aelyn want to hurt him?*" Literal asked.

"*His emotions could have just been collateral damage,*" Creativity suggested, but I knew she didn't believe it.

"*What do you actually believe?*" I asked.

They all jolted at my intrusion, but they'd have to get used to it sooner rather than later.

"*I…*" Creativity was so seldom lost for words. "*I think we're missing something. Something vital. Everyone would know how close they were. It still didn't make sense why Aelyn would just kill Jetmir.*"

"*What if it was an accident? Powerful magic directed incorrectly could kill,*" Literal added. "*Though we've not done anything dangerous with ours, so maybe we're still missing something. Plus, that doesn't make sense. If it was an accident, why write the message?*"

I addressed my Inner Child, who had gone surprisingly quiet after leading so many discussions. "*And what about you? You've been awfully quiet.*"

Her lower lip quivered a little. "*I don't care.*" Her voice was quiet. Then she said it again louder. "*I don't care! I want magic.*" I could feel my pain through her. She'd been processing and holding so much so the rest of me could think. It wasn't fair, but I also didn't know how to take it from her when she was the one who held all my memories.

"Bastien?" I tried to get his attention.

"What?" His eyes were glossy and he blinked hard against the morning sun.

"Have you seen Aelyn or Nisse this morning?" I needed someone to give answers and he was all I had.

"No. Are you looking for them?" He began scanning the crowd. "They might be down one of the side streets or moving with the parade. Though, now that you mention it, they usually join me and Jet . . . they joined us for the festival in the past."

"We should have stayed here overnight," Ronnie muttered.

"Now, why would you do that?" Bastien asked.

I scanned the crowd once more, looking for anything out of the ordinary. I needed a clue.

"*Maybe we were wrong,*" Creativity said hopefully. "*Maybe she never planned to do anything at the festival.*"

"*Or maybe she needs the parade to get here first so the square will be fuller,*" Literal suggested.

"*There,*" Inner Child screamed.

"There." I pointed. "Do you see that? The cloaked figure across the square is wearing a pendant just like the one the captor was wearing." It glinted in the morning sun.

"I don't see it," Ronnie said.

"Captor?" Bastien asked.

"You're right," Jack exclaimed.

How could we get to her without crossing the square? She stood facing the fountain, but I couldn't see her face. I scanned the surrounding crowd.

"Hilda?" I couldn't believe what I was seeing. I'd missed her at first. She'd camouflaged herself well among the flowers and decorations across the square in a small alley. No one would notice her if they weren't explicitly looking and it was clear that whatever was about to happen, she was there to watch.

"What?" Ronnie and Jack said in unison.

"There." I pointed at the concealed giantess.

"Oh, shit," Ronnie exclaimed, but she wasn't looking at Hilda.

The cloaked figure's hood slipped off. "Branson. It's been Branson this whole time," I all but whispered.

The crowd erupted in cheers that mingled with the sound of dozens of bells. The young boys of Neblig entered the square from all directions and coalesced near the fountain. They formed ranks and sang.

There was no easy way to Branson now; we'd have to shove through the crowd. This was the moment he'd strike and we'd run out of time.

I looked back where Branson was, but he was gone.

"He was just there. What is going on?" How had I lost him?

"He's fritzing." Jack furrowed his brow in determination.

"Fritzing?" I asked.

"What is that?" Ronnie asked.

"Erratic movements, disappearing and reappearing," Jack tried to explain. "There." He pointed about ten feet from where Branson had been. "That's not good. Think of it as his magic overloading itself. Right now he is holding back, but . . ." I could fill in the rest.

We followed Branson's fritzing form, but it was difficult to predict where he'd show up next. I wasn't sure what to do that wouldn't draw the crowd's attention.

"We better act quickly or he's going to do something bad," Jack said. "Even if he doesn't mean to, he will. He's appearing and disappearing more and more throughout the crowd. I don't believe he has any idea what he's messing with."

The weight of the grimoire sat heavy in my bag. I'd almost completely forgotten about it, but I couldn't pull it out in the middle of town. They would hunt me as a witch—which, though potentially true, was not something I wanted blasted out into the world. Who knows how they felt about witches in Neblig? I'd have to figure it

out without a spell book. Besides, it would take too long to look
through all the pages anyway.

Branson fritzed right in front of the crowd. Those near him
oohed and aahed as he stumbled toward the fountain. The time
for thinking had run out.

He teetered, disoriented. I don't think he even knew what he
was doing.

I had no plan. And when I looked over at Jack, he looked nervous. I could tell he didn't want to use his magic but was calcu-
lating just how bad it would be if he froze the whole town just to
move Branson out of it. The math wasn't going in the direction
he would have liked. Besides, Branson had done a number on him,
and Jack might not have the strength to do it. A half job would be
so much worse.

I reached within and tried to find my magic. I couldn't help
Branson unless I contained him. I took a step out into the square.
We could make this work, but I needed to get closer.

Branson leaned against the fountain and started to demateri-
alize. Everything slowed down, and I felt a small hand in mine.
I looked down and saw my child self looking up at me with big
doe-eyes. She smiled.

Chapter Twenty-Two

I glanced around to see if anyone else had noticed the girl show up, but they were all focused on the center of the square. No one was even watching the boys with the bells anymore. Branson had everyone's attention.

"What do we do?" I asked my Inner Child.

"What we were always meant to." She stepped forward through the crowd and pulled me along with her.

"We shouldn't go out there."

"Shhh." Inner Child put her finger to her lips. "They'll hear you."

"Don't come any closer," Branson screamed at me. Tears rolled down his cheeks. "I don't want to hurt you."

I stopped and glanced at Inner Child with questions in my eyes.

"It's a trap," she said simply.

As if to prove her point, Branson's face darkened and went slack. He glared at me. He reached up to the pendant at his neck and disappeared.

A moment later he appeared behind me, still gripping the pendant.

"Help me, please," he begged.

"Is someone controlling him?" I asked. We weren't close enough for anyone to hear except for Branson.

"Maybe that's what Hilda is there for?" Inner Child suggested, looking up at the hidden giantess.

"I don't know. She doesn't seem to be doing anything."

"Maybe it's something else then," Inner Child suggested. "Do you think that could happen to us?"

I didn't want to think about it, but it was clear I already was. "Why don't we worry about helping him right now, and we can deal with that question later?" I was painfully aware of the crowd looking at us and the longer I took, the worse it would be.

He just wants to use his magic, but he went to the wrong source. I could see myself in him. He was desperate to fit in and never did. Constantly going between Neblig and Silvaruin. How many supernatural creatures lost their magic because they feared the consequences of being exposed? My heart broke for Branson and for myself. I could grieve my past later.

"I can help you," I whispered to him, trying to coax him away from whatever had a grip on him. "I'm just like you. That's why I could do magic after I saw you. You had the pendant with you all this time." It all made sense. "It helps you with your powers, doesn't it, but it hurts you too. It makes you hurt other people." Branson's face twisted. "I never meant— This has all gone too far."

"It's alright." I took a step forward.

"I'm sorry I can't stop it." He closed his eyes and began to jitter, and his form went half corporeal. "Tell Bastien I'm sorry," his voice said, but his face was stoney calm.

Time for reason ran out. We rushed to him. Inner Child put her hand on him and brought him back.

"But I can stop it," Inner Child gasped.

He became corporeal at her touch as she became less.

She ran to me as she faded. She was barely there as she ran right into me. It was her voice alone that guided me on. *"You're right, Branson is still in there. We need to save him."* She spoke, once again inside me. I felt a bit of my energy dissipate, but it wasn't enough to do much lasting damage. *"Branson is going to disappear again. Grab the pendant."*

My eyes darted to the necklace Branson was wearing. He gripped it like a lifeline. The pendant would try to protect itself, that was clear. Like a parasite that worked against the interest of its host, it pulsed.

Branson screamed as though he were being ripped apart.

"He won't survive this," Inner Child yelled over the cries from the crowd. *"It will consume him."*

I stopped. *"Will it consume me too?"* I asked her.

"Not if we're around." A chorus of voices, my voices, went up around me, Literal, Creativity, The Originator, Sadness, and Lure. My Inner Child stayed within. The rest surrounded me.

We moved toward Branson together. Each corporeal figment grabbed a limb and held him back. They restrained him, and I lunged for his hands.

He held fast to the pendant even as it tried to destroy him. I dug my fingers under his, but he held firm. The pendant didn't want to give him up.

"I've got this," The Originator said and reached in with more strength than I currently possessed. Finger by finger, she pried Branson's grip apart. "Grab it."

The pendant was warm. Branson bucked.

Lure disappeared. Branson's leg flew free. I tugged the pendant, but I couldn't get it over his thrashing head.

Literal disappeared. He grasped for the pendant with one arm free.

Sadness disappeared. I yanked up with full force as both hands grasped for the pendant. It caught on his chin.

Creativity disappeared. He tried to pull away.

The Originator was faster. She wrapped herself around him. *"Get it off. I can't hold on much longer."*

Branson ran one direction, and I pulled the other. The pendant chain snapped and came away in my hand. The Originator disappeared.

"Drop it." Inner Child's voice came as little less than a whisper. Then again much louder, bolstered by the others, *"Drop it!"*

I threw the necklace into the water. It splashed and sank below the surface. I turned back to Branson, who looked around, confused. He trembled. Whether from fear or absence of the pendant's force, I couldn't tell.

"What is going on?" he whispered to me.

"Follow my lead," I heard myself say, and I followed the words Inner Child fed me, feeling more confident than I should have. "I have defeated the evil spirits!" My voice boomed across the square. "And now, we will usher in spring. Both of us together."

I took Branson's hand and lifted it into the air. He raised an eyebrow at me.

I mouthed, "Trust me."

"Do your thing," I said to my Inner Child. *"Please don't make a fool of me."*

Inner Child had no intention to. All around the square, people started to gasp. And for a moment I didn't know why, but then I saw them: poking up through the dirt road all around the fountain—hundreds, maybe thousands, of flowers. They grew from nothing in moments and bloomed in unison, and they were a clear message: spring had come.

The square erupted in applause, and Jack and Ronnie stepped out of the crowd and began snipping the stems and handing them out. Somehow my Inner Child knew exactly what to do. I would have been too scared of what everyone would think or do, but she just did it anyway.

I took the opportunity to whisk Branson off to the side. I had no reason to think him a continued threat, but it would be good to get him out of the square. He didn't need any more attention.

Once the flowers were cut, the rest of the plants withered to dust and became part of the road. I didn't know how I'd done it or if I'd be able to replicate such a feat, but I was proud . . . and looking at Jack, I could tell he was proud of me.

I glanced over at Hilda, who began backing away into the alley. I needed her to stay.

"*Any way we can do something about her?*" I asked Inner Child.

"*No problem,*" Inner Child responded.

I watched as vines snaked around Hilda's form, covering her ankles and wrists, then her mouth, and finally completely encasing her and obscuring her in a wall of woody plant matter. It was a light green that deepened to brown, before turning into a grey sort of stone. I really needed to figure out how I did that.

"What are you—" Branson must have been watching Hilda too.

"We need to talk. I have a feeling there is more to this story." I pulled him up on Bastien's porch. "But we'll wait until the square has cleared out."

We watched as the townsfolk dispersed with their fresh-cut flowers. One thing was clear, this was a Chalandamarz that would always be remembered.

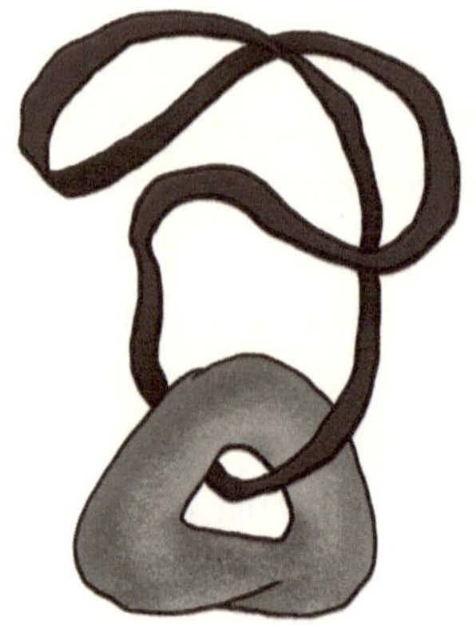

Chapter Twenty-Three

I STOOD BETWEEN BRANSON and Bastien. The fact that Bastien hadn't attacked Branson meant he hadn't put it together yet. If I could just keep things under control until the crowd completely dispersed, all would be well.

Ronnie and Jack made their way back to Bastien's shop. She went and stood beside Branson, taking my spot in making sure no one would do anything stupid, and Jack came up to me.

He pulled me into an embrace. "You were spectacular out there. I knew you had it in you."

I stood on my toes and kissed him. Our work wasn't quite finished, but I had more than enough to celebrate.

Ronnie cleared her throat. "Am I going to have to continue dealing with this?" She feigned annoyance.

"Oh yes," Jack answered before I could. "Hopefully for a long time to come."

"Why don't we see how the rest of our trip goes?" I mocked him with a noncommittal shrug, and he pulled me in tighter.

"Sorry to interrupt," Branson said, "but what happened? Is Hilda going to be alright?" He eyed the stone vines in their giantess shape.

"Hilda?" Bastien asked. "What is really going on here? Why were you moving around like that?" he asked Branson before looking at each of our faces in turn. "So I'm the only one out of the loop. Well, go on, then. Explain it all." He folded his arms and leaned back in his chair.

I didn't know where to begin. Not long ago we'd thought it was Aelyn who killed Jetmir, and now I knew it was Branson. Did I just say it outright? How would Bastien take the news?

"Have you ever seen that statue over there before?" Jack pointed at the stony vine-encased Hilda. He chose to ease into it, which was the right call.

Bastien leaned over and stared at Hilda's statue. "No, I haven't. When did that get there?"

"I put it there . . . or her, rather." I wondered if Hilda was okay. If the rock actually hurt her, I'd be no better than Branson. My body broke out in a cold sweat. I wasn't like him, not in that way.

He just looked at me expectantly, waiting for me to go on.

"She's real," I muttered. "Beneath that stoney crust, she's a real-life giantess. Magic is all around you, and Jetmir was wrapped up in it."

"I know," Bastien barked. "But why are you telling me all this? What was going on out there"—he gestured to the square, then to Branson—"with him?"

"I'm sorry," Branson began. "I didn't ever mean to hurt anyone, but I did. Jetmir tried to stop me, and I didn't listen." He hung his head. "I hurt him. I hurt him really badly, but I couldn't get help. I was addicted to trying to get my magic to work. Nothing would stand in my way, and Hilda, the giantess locked in stone, helped me every step of the way." He paused as if sharing her part in things was harder than admitting to his own. "She encouraged me, egged me on, and even put Jetmir on the top of the fountain and wrote out that sign." He shuddered and I could see a weight being lifted from him.

Bastien just stared at him. "I trusted you. Jetmir was your friend." His anger was cold, blistering beneath the surface; it was far more terrifying than explosive anger ever could be. He shook his head. "I was glad to see Jetmir getting along with someone more like him and not just me. Branson, how could you?"

"I was under some sort of compulsion. I don't know." Branson hugged his arms to his chest and wept. "I've never felt so out of control in my life. I'm sorry, Bastien. I'm sorry to you too." He nodded to Jack. "I was terrified, and you were getting close. Is Amethyst . . . ?"

"Amethyst is fine." It was clear that Jack didn't want to get into it. "Bastien, did you know about Jetmir and all the magic in Neblig?"

"Of course I knew." Bastien laughed, but it was bitter. "I let Jetmir think I didn't realize he was supernatural, but it was always clear. I just . . . I don't know, if he'd shared it with me—if I'd just asked him what was going on, he might still be here. "

"We're here if you need anything," Jack said. "But we need to deal with Branson and Hilda now, before people come back to the square."

"That's fine, I don't want any more apologies. I'm going to go inside my shop now." Bastien got up and walked to the door. "Whatever you decide to do with them is up to you. I want no part in any of this." He left without another word.

My heart hurt for him and for what this had done to his view of the supernatural world. He was one of Neblig's biggest magical supporters, and Branson had completely destroyed that. Perhaps, though, his image of magic could be rehabilitated just like Branson.

"Let's go," Jack shoved Branson down the stairs and held onto him as we crossed the square.

"*We didn't actually turn Hilda into rocks, right?*" I asked Inner Child.

But it was The Originator who answered. "*The child is resting. I'll answer. Hilda has not turned into rocks, she's merely trapped by them. I imagine she's in there screaming up a storm, but no one can hear her. Thank goodness for that.*"

"Amber?" Jack asked. "What are you thinking?"

"I don't know how to get her out. My magic is tired." I didn't think that was exactly correct, but it worked for the moment.

"Don't worry, I can help. You've done more than enough." He put his hand against one of the rough-hewn stones in front of her face, and it dissolved in a shimmer of sparks.

"Get me out of here! I'll kill her. I'll kill that bitch. I should have killed her in Silvaruin," she screamed, thrashing about in the nearly skin-tight space. In fact, it was created so close to her that she could barely move. It looked mighty uncomfortable.

"Don't dissolve more than that just yet," Ronnie said. "If she's loose, we'll all be in trouble."

"Be quiet. I might have some sympathy for Branson, but I have none for you. You knew what you were doing. So go on and explain yourself," Jack barked.

"Hilda, listen to them. I've told them enough to condemn us both." Branson didn't seem to have any fight left in him, and Hilda had enough for the both of them. Perhaps that was always how it had been.

"Branson?" Her voice was light at first, but she couldn't keep the growl away long. "How could you? You traitor."

"Did you know about that pendant, what it would do to me?" Branson asked. He dug his hand in his pocket, then pulled it back out when he realized that the pendant was gone. "It nearly consumed me out there and then what? I thought you cared."

"I do care." Hilda's voice was low and soft. "I care about you getting your magic and reaching your full potential, and you still can. Then we can take Neblig back. It is rightfully ours."

"You're demented," Branson barely whispered.

"I only did it because I care." She yelled, and it was clear she wasn't in her right mind either, but for a completely different reason from Branson. "I'm the only one you need. They aren't your friends."

"You're right, they're not—but neither are you. I am owning my part in this, and my advice is that you own yours too." He stepped back and made it clear that he was done talking to her.

"I own all of it," Hilda bellowed. "But in the end you're the one who killed Jetmir. I just used his death. Neblig is mine, the mountains are mine. They are my birthright."

"Don't you hear yourself?" I called up to her. "You used an innocent man's death for your own political ends. No matter how you spin it, you're not the good guy here."

"I did what I had to do." Her resolve was clear. There would be no remorse. Branson and Hilda could not be more different on this.

"Now what?" I asked Jack. "We can't just turn them in to the authorities. I think a giantess showing up at all would raise some eyebrows or worse. And we can't exactly explain any of it."

"Yes, unfortunately for Neblig, Jetmir's death will remain unsolved, but there isn't much we can do about that." Jack began running his hands across the stones around Hilda but in a strategic way so she couldn't break free. "I will keep Hilda in one of our rooms at the house until we can figure out what to do with her. Switzerland is a bit territorially undefined. It is definitely not my mantle's jurisdiction, but it's not really anyone else's yet. Either way, I'll handle her. As for Branson, I think I'm going to try and work with him. If what he says is true, I think I can help him. He will have to see justice, but afterward, I might be able to help him."

He glanced over at Branson who stood near Hilda's foot, and I could see he was thinking about his sister. Jack wanted to help, and that was a feeling I knew all too well.

I stood back and let him work on Hilda while I kept an eye on Branson. I didn't think he'd run, but it was never wrong to be careful.

"You did a really good job with these stones," Jack remarked as he finished binding her limbs and releasing her from the rocks. "I guess you've progressed from flowers. That's a good sign."

"It might not be progression," Ronnie said, dashing my hopes.

"What do you mean?"

"I've read your book." Ronnie still didn't realize my dismay. "Wasn't it about a girl who was part flower and part rock? Flourin and Petrian or something like that?"

"Yes, but I don't . . . oh!" I don't know if Inner Child helped me understand. "You're saying my magic is based on my stories?"

Ronnie shrugged.

"It's a good explanation," Jack said as he hefted Hilda over his shoulder, which was ridiculously impressive as she stood significantly taller than him and was much stockier. "I'll have to do some research on it though. Creation and magic are heavily tied, but this is a new one for me."

"Great, so I'm a freak of nature." I laughed.

"We all are." Jack smiled, then said, "Come on, let's get out of town before someone sees me with a giant on my shoulder."

I tried to make sense of everything in the day, but it was proving difficult. I'd done magic on my own and saved Branson, but I still felt so far behind. Perhaps I was doomed to feel that way forever.

And what about the pendant? What was that? There were still questions. I'd have to see if I could collect it from the fountain. Perhaps it could be useful and not just a tool of destruction—or maybe it was tempting me just like Branson.

Chapter Twenty-Four

We reentered Neblig to the sound of singing. It wasn't for us; it was for spring. Everyone had eaten well and gone to a large dance hall to celebrate spring. And this year, I had a feeling the festivities would be even more joyous than usual, and I had somehow entered that lore.

"Let me get this straight," Jack said. "You want to go fishing in the fountain for the pendant that nearly drove Branson mad? Are you insane?"

"I might be soon." It wasn't really that strange. "We should get it out, though; that's not the sort of thing you want just lying around."

"I guess, but you shouldn't touch it."

"Do you know what it is?" Ronnie asked. She'd stopped at one of the vendors and was already sipping a beer. I had a feeling that the festivities weren't ready for her.

"It's likely a seer stone. They are extraordinarily powerful and can turn a person mad. They have different effects on different types of humans and supernaturals, and each stone is different too. Some of them have histories and titles like swords do. But there are likely many that have no history to their names. Whatever that one is, it did not work well with Branson, that's for sure."

We wound our way toward the center of town, and I was grateful that most people were still off celebrating. It would be strange fishing in the fountain with people watching.

"If we find it, we should leave it at Bastien's until after the festival," Jack said. "It's not a good idea to have it on you."

"And Branson had it in his pocket all this time?" I thought aloud. "All the unexplained magical happenings were because of him." I shivered. That could so easily be me, and if I was right, all my breakthroughs were because of the pendant and nothing else. I'd combed back through everything that had happened in Neblig as we walked up to Jack's house and realized each time I'd used magic, I'd come into contact with Branson and the pendant, even the night where I saw my face in the fire.

"You do realize it might not hurt you like it did to Branson." I could feel him beginning to enable me.

"And how will I know?"

"We'll figure it out together." He took my hand. "There are plenty of books about these things, and I have two very old libraries and quite a few ancient, primary sources."

The conversation died as we made it to the fountain. I could see the silver rock and its glimmering chain below the churning water. I didn't want to get too wet because there was no way I was climbing back up the mountain again to get changed.

The water grew clear, and I looked up to see Jack had put a piece of wood above me to block the spray, so I could reach in and get the pendant. I leaned forward and the water distorted. Before me lay a field of poppies. I turned around and saw the wall, only this time I turned around and the crack in the wall had crumbled into a hole.

Child me rushed to the hole and peered through. I could hear yelling from the house, and there was my mother yelling at a man. I snuck into the garden with its neat rows of daisies. Everything was in perfect order, except the couple yelling on the porch.

"Go," my mom screamed at him. "She's just like you."

He rushed to his car, and my mom slammed the door. Then he doubled back and came up behind me in the garden. He must have known I was there the whole time.

"Hey, little one." That was what he called me. "You need to be careful. I won't be here to stand up for you anymore. She'll take it out on you. I'm sorry I couldn't do more."

"Daddy, take me with you," I whispered, afraid to even wish it. He wasn't the father I grew up with, but I knew he was my dad.

"I wish I could, but I'll come back. I promise. Until then, I'll keep you safe the only way I know how." He kissed me on the forehead.

My whole body filled with warmth. In moments, though, I felt frozen, and he'd disappeared into the night.

The memory dissipated with a splash. I turned toward the sound and saw Ronnie with the chain dangling from her cloth-covered hand.

"What are you—" I spluttered.

"No, what are you doing? What just happened there?" Ronnie asked as she tucked the pendant into a little leather pouch that I hadn't even realized she'd pulled from my hip.

"I saw my dad. He left when I was a kid." Tears rolled down my cheeks. He left me, and he took a piece of me with him. I had so many things to grieve and all I wanted to do was give my Inner Child a hug. She had to hold so much pain.

"Your parents are still together though, right?" Ronnie asked, confused.

"No, my real father. I must have blocked it out, or maybe I was too young to remember." I sobbed. "I don't know why he would have left. I wanted to go with him. I don't know where he went, and he said he'd come back, but he never did."

Ronnie dropped the pouch and pulled me into a hug. "It's alright. Maybe this is your next mystery to unravel. But for now, just let me hold you."

"Maybe he couldn't come back." Deep sadness clouded Jack's voice. "Maybe he had a job to do, something that a child couldn't participate in or understand."

"What do you mean?" I pulled out of Ronnie's arms. "What do you mean?"

"He's the supernatural one, right?" he asked.

"I would assume so."

"Then he might have responsibilities, like I do. I used to not control much, but B gave me a lot more responsibilities." He sighed. "There are things I cannot do. There are times when I must be in places I don't want to be. I am an integral part of nature, and maybe your dad is too."

"You're saying he might be like you?" I swallowed hard.

"It is likely." Jack picked up the leather pouch and carried it as we walked toward Bastien. "Whatever power you have is strong. There are very few beings that would produce such power, especially when mixed with a human."

I felt like I was choking after finally finding my foothold and starting to feel alright. Jack ran inside Bastien's shop to drop off the pendant and came back out as Ronnie was hugging me again. I was so grateful she'd come with me. I couldn't have done all this alone.

"Do you need a moment, or should we head to the party?" he asked.

"I should be alright by the time we get there." I wasn't sure if that was true at all, but I hoped that it was.

The singing grew louder as we got closer to the hall, and I focused on it. Now was not a time for weeping but for celebration.

We'd saved Branson from himself, and in a way, we'd saved Neblig and Silvaruin even if they didn't know it.

Jack took my hand as we stepped up to the door, and Ronnie, not to be outdone, took my other one. I took a little courage and strength from each of them, and we went in together.

The crowd went wild when they saw me, and I wanted to shrink away to nothing. They spoke in multiple languages and I didn't understand them, but I could tell they were happy and had had plenty to drink before I got there.

"Come on," Jack said and pulled me onto the dance floor. "They'll insist and I might as well lead."

"I don't know the steps." I really didn't feel like dancing. Then I looked over at Ronnie, who had found a partner as she did so easily. She did this stuff with a kind of grace I could only dream of. After all, she was the same elven warrior I'd met in the forest of Coldwater; grace was in her essence.

"Just look in my eyes, and you'll be fine."

I focused back on Jack's piercing blue eyes with their half-gray slant. He truly was handsome in a cutting sort of way. He had sharp features, and his long blond hair flowed and danced along with his movements. Warmth spread across my chest, and I found myself smiling as I followed his lead through the dance.

"You are magnificent." He grinned at me, but I didn't let it distract my foot pattern.

"And your hands are cold."

"A hazard of my trade, unfortunately."

"I'll warm them up." Lure did a somersault in my stomach.

We danced until I felt my feet would fall off, and in the end my heart was full.

We finally left the dance floor and I said, "I'm glad you're helping Branson."

"Yeah, why's that?"

"He's like me." I didn't mention his sister, but I thought about her.

Nobody but me noticed when Bastien showed up. I don't know why, but I expected him to be more angry. Then again, he knew someone killed Jetmir, and learning who didn't change his amount of pain.

"I think you should go talk to Bastien. He needs friends right now." I pushed him in that direction, and he didn't protest.

I went to go find Ronnie. She was drinking some punch with Aelyn and Nisse. Something still bothered me. Aelyn had been hiding something. The fact that I hadn't uncovered it frustrated me.

". . . oh, I imagine waterfalls are much different from rivers," Ronnie said as I came up. "All that churning must affect your personality."

"I don't know what you're talking about," Nisse said with obvious sarcasm. "Aelyn is the calmest woman I've ever met. No chaotic energy at all."Aelyn slapped him on the shoulder. "Quit giving the wrong idea." Then I saw it. The slight too-hard hit and anger deep in her eyes.

"Why did you try to kill your husband?" I blurted out.

"Pardon?" Aelyn asked.

Nisse looked from her to me in slow motion. "What is the meaning—"

"Why don't you tell him." I nodded. "It wasn't Branson that poisoned the buns, it was you. Only you weren't lying when you said you didn't mean to hurt Amethyst. You really meant to hurt Nisse, only it didn't hurt him because he's human. You had a bun on your hike, didn't you Nisse?"

"I did." He backed away from her.

She opened her mouth to explain. But Ronnie cut in instead, and I was more than happy to have them figure that out on their own. "You and B seem to be getting on well." I was glad she remembered to use his nickname. "I'm sure the whole town can see how in love you are."

I blushed, but I couldn't deny it. I'd already done so for long enough.

Chapter Twenty-Five

MY HEART FLUTTERED EVERY time I saw Jack, and I grew sad knowing I had to leave him. His words about needing to be in certain places at certain times weighed heavy on my heart. Even extending our stay an extra couple of weeks wasn't enough. I had so much to learn and too little time to spend with him.

He promised to write about Branson's progress because we knew it would help me too. He planned to find any excuse to send me a letter, but distance was difficult. I wished I hadn't been so distracted and hadn't taken things slow. Yet I still knew it was the right thing to do.

Hilda never gave us any more information, even though Branson went and visited and talked to her for a few hours every day. It was as though she had completely shut down. And I tried to update my blog but didn't know how. It was predicated on clearing the name of the supernatural, but now I had to rethink that entirely. Perhaps some things were better kept hidden, at least specific details.

I had to try to tell the world, but in a safe way.

If there is any lesson that repeatedly kicks me in the teeth, it is the lesson of how little I understand. Understanding is different from knowing. I know a lot of things, but I understand far too little.

I believe my perspective will be ever-changing. It has changed over the last couple of weeks that I've been neglecting this blog (I'm sorry about that BTW), but sometimes life just gets in the way.

Perhaps I will write more when I've had time to process everything, or maybe I'll explore this through fiction. That is, after all, my first love.

Thank you for caring, and still believe with all your heart,
Amber.

I closed my blog draft and pulled up Nessi's story. The blog might just stay there for a while before being deleted. If Nessi really had helped with my magic, I couldn't give up on her story.

Nessi and Beast trudged into the human camp. Every step of the journey felt like a mile. She stumbled to the ground in front of the first tent where she'd met the boy, token squeezed tight in her palm even though she didn't need it.

Beast howled. "Help, please. Is there anyone there?"

Nessi faded in and out of consciousness, feeling hands and movement but not knowing what was really going on.

Then a woman's voice whispered in her ear, "Nessi, darling, you're hurt, but we will mend you, body and soul."

Nessi wondered if the woman was the one who had spoken to her from the fire or if maybe she was her real mother. That was something she'd never considered. She had a real mother.

I shut my computer on the draft. Jack and Ronnie were probably already ready to go. I didn't feel good about leaving, but we'd extended our trip as long as it was feasible to stay away. But one whole season hadn't felt like enough.

The truth was, we still had more to do in Coldwater.

"Ah, there you are," Ronnie said as I rolled my suitcase down the hall. "I was just about to go drag you from your room kicking and screaming."

I didn't respond. I wasn't in a joking mood. I would have preferred to kick and scream, but it was time.

"We're going to miss you," Amethyst said and patted my leg. "You'll have to visit us again soon, and don't just write to Jack and forget me."

"I won't. I promise." It was a promise I intended to keep.

I went over to Jack and gave him a kiss.

"You realize I'm coming with you to the station, right?" He smiled.

"And I can't just kiss you because I want to?"

He laughed. "Of course you can. Come on, then." He grabbed Ronnie's and my suitcases and headed outside. He'd given me a few things: two of his shirts and a thick sweater he'd worn the last couple of days, and a bottle of his cologne.

Goodbyes were always difficult, but even more so when the person you cared for only communicated by mail.

"You should really get a phone or maybe a laptop," I pushed for the umpteenth time.

"I would only use it for you."

"Am I not enough?" I batted my eyes and generally looked foolish.

He laughed. "I'll find a way to communicate with you better. I promise."

I tried not to let Lure run away with travel plans, wedding plans, kids' names, and all the rest, but she was difficult to combat after letting her take a little bit of the reins.

We arrived at the station just as the train came in. I wished for five more minutes, but it wouldn't have made a difference because I still would have had to say goodbye.

Jack set down our suitcases and pulled me to him. He gave me a long kiss. I wanted to stay in that moment forever, with my heart intact, but time is cruel and keeps on going.

"I love you, Amber."

"And I love you, Jack."

"And I love that you love each other," Ronnie said.

The train whistle sounded.

"I'm going to miss you," I said.

"I'll miss you more."

Ronnie picked up our bags and ushered me onto the train. There was no other way I was leaving. It was silly perhaps, but I'd fallen for Jack.

I watched him from the window as the train pulled out of the station and wished he were coming with me. Once he was out of view, I felt my heart start to unravel. Even the beauty of the Swiss Alps wasn't enough to distract me, so I turned back to my blog. Perhaps there was another way to vent my feelings.

Nothing is as it seems, not even me. There are certain journeys you shouldn't take alone. I am glad of the friends I have made in my travels and hope to make many more. Would you believe me if I told you I've met some of the creatures I told you about in my last blog? Well, you should. Because I did.

I like to put people and things into nice, easy, definable boxes, but that is so rarely the case. I thought I'd gotten better at that. You would think that believing in magic would stretch me to a point where boxes were irrelevant, but I think too much in black and white.

Anyone can do the wrong thing if they feel they have the right reason. Motivations are fickle, and so are memories. I've learned a lot about giants and undines, and myself.

But enough of my soap box. You're here for magical creatures.

We found a giantess, though she wasn't as large as Old Gargy and his daughters. Those giants remain hidden if they are still around.

I met an Undine; her clothing felt wet even when it was perfectly dry, and she was quite a good hostess.

I met a kobold who cooks better than anyone I know and is feisty yet kind.

Perhaps one day I will put all that I've found in a book to share with the world, but I'll keep my newfound friends private for safety.

But for those out there reading this, believe with your whole heart and cut your own path,

Amber.

Writing the blog post didn't heal my heart completely, but it did help. Ronnie was already asleep on my shoulder. I honestly didn't know how she did it. That left me with my thoughts and a window full of stunning views.

My mind wandered, and I wondered just where the next few years might take me. I knew Jack and I would work on figuring out who my father was, but I wasn't holding out much hope.

The seer-stone pendant weighed heavy in the bag on my hip. Jack told me it was safe to keep. And Ronnie told me she'd steal it from me if I went too far.

My mind might be locked, but the pendant might just be the key.

Acknowledgments

First and foremost, I want to thank my writing group who have helped me to grow in extraordinary ways. They are my rock upon which the scaffolding of my stories have taken shape. I want to thank my beta readers who have donated their time and brainpower to making this book fit to print. I want to thank my editor, Lynda Dietz, for polishing up my grammar, punctuation, and sentence structure. And, last but not least, I want to thank my family who support me in my insatiable need to sit at a computer and hallucinate worlds into existence.